Jackpot!

What happens to a man when he hits the jackpot? Wins millions on the pools, the national lottery?

Irascible Kenneth Wicks was from honest, working-class stock, a drayman in a brewery, with a loving mother and sister and expectant fiancée.

Then the miracle happened: riches beyond dreams; big house, fast car, fast girls, booze unlimited, free days, parties in London . . .

After one such, driving home after a night in the nick, fuming at the world and all authority – he'd get back at them! – he stopped at a favourite spot in the forest to savour the peace of the place, only to find a decrepit figure profaning the sacred spot, begging the price of a drink.

When Kenneth had taken his hands from the man's throat the wretch was dead. But so what? No evidence, no witness, no motive – just a silly old tramp whom someone had strangled.

But it wasn't easy. Guilt does strange things to a man, and when Kenneth was unfortunate enough to meet in his local the wise, acutely perceptive Chief Superintendent George Gently – local celebrity meets local celebrity – his luck began to falter . . .

Jackpot! is a *tour de force* of sustained perfection.

Also by Alan Hunter

JACKPOT!

Alan Hunter

Constable · London

First published in Great Britain 1995
by Constable & Co Ltd
3 The Lanchesters, 162 Fulham Palace Road
London W6 9ER
Copyright © 1995 by Alan Hunter
The right of Alan Hunter to be identified
as the author of this work has been
asserted by him in accordance with
the Copyright, Designs and Patents Act 1988
ISBN 0 09 475100 5
Set in Linotron Palatino 10pt by
CentraCet Ltd, Cambridge
Printed and bound in Great Britain by
Hartnolls Ltd, Bodmin

A CIP catalogue record for this book
is available from the British Library

1

He scribbled his name. He shoved the form across the desk. The sergeant handed him the bag containing his possessions. As he crammed them back into his pockets the sergeant watched him with a calculating eye.

'And if you've got any sense at all . . .'

He could have hit the bugger. Why didn't he?

'If you've got any sense at all you'll try to pull yourself together, my lad.'

Yes, he should have hit him, sent him reeling: there were only the two of them in reception. They'd have re-arrested him, of course, and thrown him back into that stinking cell. But so what? Police persecution! And he could buy enough law to make it stick. Didn't they realize yet who they were dealing with, after all the enquiries they'd made?

Nearly, so nearly, he'd hit that bugger. But instead he'd merely glared, turned his back, lurched out into the street. Christ he had a head! How much had he drunk? The noise of the traffic seemed to drill into his brain. He needed a drink, but where to get one at this time of day in bloody London? If you did find a pub . . .

In the end he pushed through the door of a small café.

'Give me a black coffee.'

The girl had stared at him as she served it. She ventured: 'You look a bit rough, lovey!'

'Never mind that!' He fumbled for a note. The girl took it, but then shook her head.

'Can't change this, lovey.'

7

He'd given her a fifty. With an effort, he searched in his pocket and came up with a pound coin.

He drank the coffee and ordered another. He'd been on Scotch . . . and that bloody tart. Had he hit her? He couldn't remember, just a vision of collapsing tables, drinks flying, screaming, shouting, some sod grabbing him. Then the police, the wagon, the cell.

'All this money – where did you get it from?'

Had he managed to tell them? Well, they must have found out! He'd got it all back, it was there in the bag, the stuffed wallet, the roll of fifties.

Not that it mattered a blind cuss.

In the safe at the hotel, the nearest bank . . .

Sod them all. Sod London. Was this the way to treat a bloke like him?

He ordered a third coffee.

'Keep the bloody change!'

'Look . . . do you know what you've given me?'

'You heard me – keep it!'

But the coffee was working on him, clearing his brain. What it wasn't doing was slaking the fire of his resentment. He'd come here in good faith, come for a good time. Come with his pockets full. And they'd treated him like dirt. A night in the cells – him, the winner, the man with it all! Who could have bought the bloody hotel, pensioned off the scum who'd arrested him. Sod them. Sod them. They needed a lesson. At least, back home, they knew who they were dealing with.

But what was the bloody use . . .?

He gulped back the coffee and headed for the door.

'Here . . . I've got your change!'

'Then you know what you can do with it!'

In the street he had to think which way he must go to get back to the hotel. Take a taxi? In that sodding traffic it would be quicker on foot. But where was he? He had to ask. He didn't know to which police station the bastards had taken him. It must have been half an hour later when he reached the ornate foyer of the hotel.

8

And of course the sods there were waiting for him . . .

'We must ask you to leave this hotel, Mr Wicks. Your luggage has been packed and placed in your car, and if you will be kind enough to pay this estimated bill . . .'

Why bloody argue? He paid it. They returned the fat envelope he'd deposited in the safe. Then they accompanied him down to the basement garage where the Jag was waiting with the key in the ignition. He climbed in, belted up, set the smooth engine rolling. Through the window, he tossed a fifty to the attendant. And drove out of that bloody place.

If he'd been stopped the police must have nicked him: he was in no state to drive a car. Luckily the morning rush was slackening and he hit the A12 without too much aggro. Perhaps it was the soothing influence of the car, the Jag which had been one of his earliest acquisitions, bought from Mann Egerton in Norchester with a cheque which they'd had to refer before accepting it. Well, he'd turned up in his old suit driving an Escort fit only for the scrap yard . . . who was he to be test-driving a Jag with a twenty-seven thousand price-ticket? But the cheque hadn't bounced and they'd allowed him a silly price for the Escort. And driving home he'd hit the ton in one or two places.

Disappointingly, his mother had been doubtful about it, while Joyce . . . it was no good, he would never understand her! So he may have kicked over a bit when it happened, but wasn't that natural, would have happened with anybody? A bit of a booze-up with the lads and a couple of tarts. So bloody what?

He noticed the speedo and eased his foot – that was the trouble with the Jag! It was too smooth, too casual, you were drifting into the nines before you realized it.

Then – there was the house. All right, he'd gone overboard! It was too big, too old, needed lashings spent on it. But that was small change now. He could have swept it bare, refurnished from scratch, done every repair from cellar to roof. So why didn't they like it, his obstinate mother, his girl-friend still living with her family at home? Either could have been mistress of the old manse with its many bedrooms and vast living space ... instead of which he was stuck there alone, with a daily housekeeper from the village. He'd had no heart to spend on the place, other than repairs to the leaking roof.

Perhaps it was his mother who disappointed him most. From the start, she would have nothing to do with his money. Wanted to go on living in her bungalow in Wolmering as though nothing, but nothing, had happened. Father's pension was enough, it would see out her time. No, she didn't want any stupid annuity. The most she would allow was a new fridge and and a new stove – even modest double-glazing she couldn't be bothered with.

Well, his sisters hadn't been so stand-offish! To each he had donated a hundred thou. Gwen, wife of a commercial travel-ler, Dick Adams, now owned her smart house in Walderness. The other two lived further off and he didn't know what they were doing with theirs, but they certainly hadn't rejected it. Like his mother. Like Joyce.

But Joyce he would never understand ...

Only, the wedding next spring was off.

He checked his speed again: a low eighty. He was approach-ing the Orwell Bridge. Soon, perhaps too soon, he was going to be back in that lonely house. To do ... what? Christ knew! He hadn't let Vera know he'd be back. He'd have lunch out somewhere, if he could face lunch, then spin out the time till evening opening. Wasn't it just to escape this that he'd fled the house, the village, had aimed himself and his money at the capital, determined to live, to live it up, to get some meaning out of existence? And it had lasted just two days – after two days he'd been treated like dirt! Kenneth Wicks and his multi-millions ... Surely there was a way ... some way ...?

He drove over the bridge, reached the junction, struck the A12 again. Not many miles now! Not much after noon he would be back in Welbourne village. He could press on and visit his sister, invite her out to lunch. Or his mother. But somehow he found himself shrinking from either alternative. What would he tell them? That he'd spent the night in jail and been slung out of his hotel? He could imagine his mother's face . . . or his sister's if it came to that! The Wickses were honest, honest working-class. His father had been a post-office sorter. He himself had worked as a drayman at the brewery before his win. And Joyce, she was manageress in the small town's supermarket . . . not that he intended lunching with Joyce! No: just now, he must stay on his own . . .

He overtook crazily, nearly hit a truck, left a horn blaring somewhere behind him. So frigging what! The rules were for lesser men, not for the drivers of ton-plus Jags. All the same he eased off again, dropped his speed to an arguable seventy-five. He would get there plenty soon enough, no need to go scaring the reps and old ladies. His head was aching. He needed a drink. But still it was half an hour to opening. Coming to a village, he hesitated, but then renewed pressure on the throttle. What was the use? Sod them all! Cops, people, relatives, the whole lousy bag . . .

He came to a turn-off to the village, but for some reason let it go. He needed a break, a moment to think, before he showed up there again. He thought of the forest. Why not? He could find a parking there in the shade: yes, a moment to cool off before he had to pick up with his life again. So he took the next turning, cut his speed to a crawl, let the Jag amble amiably towards the distant reef of trees.

The forest was special. He had known it as a kid, when they'd gone there on Sunday picnics – mum, dad, the girls, himself, driving in dad's old Super Minx. They would park in the shade of a ride and get out the folding chairs and table; then, while mum was setting out the picnic, he and the girls would charge about through the trees. Of course, it had changed now. That favourite spot had been levelled by the hurricane. Now there was a different picnic area, rather more developed, set in a clearing on the other side of the road. He drifted through trees, pine sections edged with hardwoods,

11

found the spot quite deserted and bumped the Jag into a pool of shade. Yes! He climbed out. The fragrance, the sounds: still the same. Bloody money, what did it buy you? He leaned against the car and took deep breaths.

But he wasn't quite alone there either. He heard movement and, frowning, stared across at a picnic table on the edge of the clearing. A decrepit figure squatted there. A tramp in a filthy coat, tied up with rope. He had a bundle beside him and was eating a sandwich which he'd taken from a paper bag. Sod him, did he have to be there? Wicks felt a surge of hot anger. He jerked his gaze away, stared into the trees, jammed his hands in his pockets. He wanted that place on his own! He wanted to be alone to think. He tried hard to forget that disreputable figure, to shut his ears to the rustle of the paper bag. But it wasn't to be. He heard the tramp burp, heard him wiping his hands on the bag. Then he heard a shuffle of steps towards him, found himself staring at an old, whiskered face.

'Could you spare the price of a drink, guv?'

Words wouldn't come. His hands spoke for him. He pulled out notes, held them in a fan, shoved them under the tramp's nose. The man stared at them. Then at him. Then he advanced a trembling hand. At that moment the notes fell scattering and Wicks's hands had closed on the tramp's throat. Exultation! He was heavy, he fell. Yet still he was profaning that sacred spot. But only yards away was the sunken water-tank installed by the Forestry in case of fire. Safety netting, it had to be pulled back, further, further, and then ... The bundle, too – it wouldn't sink, so bloody what? – and the netting pulled back, hooked tight. Then the notes, some tossed in the breeze ... the paper bag: shove it under the brambles! There. There. There. The spot was clean. And he was alone.

Had it happened? It must have done! He found himself back beside the Jag. He was sweating, breathing hard, his head pounding madly. So what, so bloody what? Who cared a toss for scum like that? What did it matter? If they found him, they weren't going to pull out many sodding stops!

And now he was square. Square with those bastards. Square for the night he'd spent in a cell. Kenneth multi-million Wicks: square with the bloody universe.

He got back in the car and sat a while. Then belted up and drove.

'If you'd let me know . . . are you feeling all right, now?'

The house had been shut up and it smelled: smelled of age and ancient things, of the old lady who had lived there before he bought it.

She had been someone well-known, the widow of a minister, and had carried on there till her nineties. Once or twice, when he'd been delivering at the Bell, he had seen her crossing the green with her two Scotch terriers. 'You know who *she* is?' the landlord had asked him, and he'd stared again at that majestic figure. Well, now *he* owned the house. He'd bought it from her heirs, who just wanted to be rid of it.

'You do look poorly, Mr Kenny.'

'I shall be all right, Vera.'

'There isn't very much in the house. If you'd let me know . . .'

'I'm not hungry.'

'I can do you a fry-up. There's some bacon and an egg.'

She'd seen his car pull up, of course, and come trotting over from her cottage across the green: Vera Wilson, his soft-spoken little pensioner, with her pallid, creased face and misty eyes. She was younger than his mother, but not much. Her husband had been a council road-worker. She did her work for him conscientiously – but then, he paid her over the odds. Now her eyes were worried.

'If you're quite sure . . .'

'Just don't worry about me, Vera.'

'Perhaps you didn't get much sleep . . .'

Was something really showing in his face?

She went. He stood for a moment, watching her cross the green again. Then he went to stare in the old gilt-framed

13

mirror that hung beside the coat-stand in the hall. Just the hangover, that was all! Eyes a bit bloodshot, cheeks puffy. A heavy-looking face, not handsome, broad jaw, eyes sunken, a hooked nose. Oh, to hell! Women liked him. His wiry brown hair. And he was only thirty. Lots of time ... No, there was nothing showing in his face.

He growled to himself and went through to the kitchen in search of a can of beer. Perhaps he did feel peckish after all, and there was cheese in the fridge and half a pork pie. He sat down with them at the kitchen table. Surprisingly, yes, he did have an appetite. He added a couple of bananas to the feast and ate greedily till he'd cleared the plates. That was better! He drained the beer. So he'd been a bloody fool, but that was all – nothing that stuck, nothing that showed. And not a damned thing they could pin on him. The whole sodding deal could have been a dream, a part of the hangover, no more. So!

He shoved his plates in the sink and went to the telephone in the hall.

'Mum?'

A pregnant pause. 'Oh, it's you then, is it? So where have you been?'

'Just a trip into town.'

'A trip into town. And not a word to anyone!'

He felt for a chair, and sat.

'And what were you doing up there, I wonder?'

'Oh, go on, mum! It was just a trip.'

'Yes, and I know what your trips are like. What sort of trouble have you been in this time?'

'No . . . trouble at all.'

'Yes, that's what you say!'

'I tell you, it was just a trip. I felt like it, you know, a change. I felt I was getting into a bit of a rut.'

'A bit of a rut.' He could hear her grunt. 'You didn't use to talk that way once, son. But then you had a job and things to do, you didn't have time to get into ruts.'

'Oh, mum!'

'And don't oh mum me. I tell you, my son, you're doing

yourself no good. That stupid money has gone to your head, you're only half the man you were once. Do you hear me?'

'Yes, I hear you – '

'Only half the man, I say. And I can't think what your father would have said if he'd known of your carryings-on. You used to be a good boy, Kenny. You did your job, looked after your old mother. And there's Joyce too, what about her? Have you never thought how you're letting her down?'

'Mum . . . I still want to marry her!'

'But does she want to marry you? Not if she's got any sense she doesn't! You can't dazzle her with your silly money.'

What was the use? He held the phone from his ear, but could still hear her voice rabbiting on. Nothing would change her. Hadn't he always been the odd one out in the family? It was the girls who had her attention, the little club of his sisters, their dresses, their secrets, friends, a mystique he had no part in. He was the youngest . . . and a boy. An outsider. A nuisance. Always he got the sharp edge of her tongue, could do no right, and they no wrong. Desperately, he replaced the phone.

'Listen, mum – just listen! It could all be so different if you would only give me a chance. We could do this place up. It's big, there's plenty of room. You could come here, and Joyce, and we could really make a go of it. You'd have help in the house, we could have a gardener, anything you can think of. I don't want to live like this. Why can't you just give it a chance?'

'A chance he says!'

'Yes – a chance, instead of always running me down. At least you could do that. It isn't such a lot to ask.'

'I see. I'm to live like a lady.'

'To live like – any way you want!'

'And what would you be doing, my son?'

'Me? Well, I'd find something . . .!'

'Yes, I'm sure.' Her voice was tart. 'And you expect me to go along with all that.'

'You don't understand – '

15

'Oh yes I do, Kenny. No one knows you better than me. And I won't stand for it, you hear me? First, I would have to be sure of you.'

'But mum – '

'You heard me.'

'Oh . . . what's the use!'

He heard her fiddle with the receiver. 'Son, I'm going to tell you straight. It's time for you to pull yourself together.'

'That's – the second time I've heard that today!'

'Then this time you'd better listen. Since you won that money you haven't been yourself, it's driven you right off the rails.'

'But . . . what do you want?'

'I want you, my son, to try to be the man you used to be. To get an honest job, to make it up with Joyce, to settle down to living a decent life. Is that such a lot to ask?'

'But I don't need a job!'

'Oh yes you do. Nobody more so.'

'But why? Why?'

'If you don't know that, then there's no point in my talking to you any longer.'

'But mum . . .'

'No point. So just you think about it. And now I've got to go up to the shops.'

The phone went dead. He sat hugging the receiver. Then he slammed it down with a savage cry.

Suddenly the money was aching in his pocket – he was a sodding millionaire, wasn't he? Then he could spend, spend, spend, no way he could ever get through all that. What could he buy? Something! – but what? House, car, clothes, he'd got them, spent a couple of thou on a bloody watch, another thou on a camera. The trouble was he hadn't been brought up to money, didn't know the proper ways to get rid of it. A pair of guns, say? But where would he use them? A horse? But he didn't ride. A yacht he'd considered in the first flush, then given it up as too much of a bind. And travel didn't interest him, so why buy a load of that? No. There was nothing that came to mind. Nothing he could throw a handful of notes at. He'd tried bloody London . . . tried! Booze and bints seemed all that was left for him.

Then the frenzy faded and he was remembering – oh hell, oh bloody hell! He stared at his hands, large, hairy . . . had he washed the buggers when he came in? It wasn't, couldn't have been him back there. He'd watched some other sod do it. Or some other sod had taken over, used him, made him his bloody tool. It was unreal, didn't happen, was just something he'd dreamed when the fellow stood before him – that must be it. It was all in his mind. A dream, a phantasm, the last kick of his hangover. Only then . . . on his hand was a bloody scratch, received when he dragged that netting back over. So, so. So! So he'd bloody done it, what then? He hadn't meant to, never would have if those sods in London hadn't treated him like muck. It was their lousy fault, not his, let them have it on their conscience . . .

He sprang up and went out of the house, leaving the door unlocked behind him, the Jaguar unlocked in the drive – what did he care for any bastard? He strode over the green, took the road that would lead him to the heath, the heath now purple in August, the heath that was fringed by the forest . . . To go back there? No, sod it, sod it! Just to be alone, to walk. To let his mind recover itself. To get back to where he was before he went to London. So he strode out down the half-mile of road to the purple slopes and their yellow cushions of dwarf gorse.

Here too he had come with the family when he was a kid in short trousers, his sisters in summer dresses, the eldest almost a woman. There, unchanged, was the bumpy pull-off where his dad always parked the Super Minx, the bit of rough brackeny ground where they set up for the picnic. Then, it had seemed so far from the forest. The forest belonged to a different day. By road it was at least two miles, though across the heather . . . he turned his eyes away! Yes, across there, perhaps a quarter of a mile, lay the dark line of the pines, through which – he knew the location – ran the ride to the picnic area. He glanced again. Oh, bugger! What was he expecting, the cops already? Police cars, uniform men, their eyes turned to the figure on the road? Hell, it might be weeks, months before anyone took a look in the tank ... it was suddenly before his eyes, brambles, willow-herb growing all round it. No! In a couple of blue moons someone might check the water level, but no more. It could be years before what was there came to light ...

Still, he wanted his back to those trees. He walked on till there was access to the heath on the opposite side, and there climbed over a locked gate and set off along a track between two slopes. It led by an old, abandoned gravel extraction, which soon put the forest out of sight, also the parked cars, the visitors: here, he had the heath to himself. He walked, made his mind a blank. He didn't *have* to think about that! He gazed at the heather, the occasional bushes, the rabbits that scuttled away at his approach. He was back again. Back before *that*. Kenny Wicks who, six months ago ... In the village they knew, or guessed, but had no way of telling how much. He was back, and he was going to stay back. All that had happened to some other. One day, some day, mum would give in, and Joyce ... well, if not her, then another ... He walked and walked. But it had to happen: the track was rising to a summit in the heath. At last, slowly, he turned about and remained, his eyes riveted on that dark line of trees. Then, with a wrenching groan, he threw himself down in the bracken and lay, with his arm across his face, hearing only the note of an unknown bird.

Cramp roused him at last from his stupor, that and a feeling of chillness and damp. The sun was low, was reddening, and mist beginning to form in the hollows. He looked at his watch ... yes, evening. The world had turned since he dropped down there. Had moved on. Things must have been happening. Slowly he stretched and sat up. Well ... if they'd been looking for him! But no, it was too soon. No need for him to skulk out there with the chill creeping into his bones. He got gingerly to his feet, stood a moment gazing at the empty heath; then shook his head stupidly and set off in the direction of the village. He had to behave ... well, normally! Like a man with nothing on his mind at all. He'd had a bad dream, but now it was over, left behind there on the misted heath. So then? When he reached the village, after a pause, he turned his steps towards the Bell.

'You're back, then!'

'Yes ... I'm back.'

Had Sid, the landlord, looked at him oddly? He reached at once for a pint tankard and adroitly filled it with bitter.

'Vera was in here earlier. She said you got back about lunchtime. Said you were looking a bit rough. Here, get this down you, it'll cheer you up.'

He took the tankard and drank. Around him in the bar were the usual faces. Most were the affluent elderly who made up a large part of the village population. They regarded him curiously, perhaps a little contemptuously: he had never yet felt properly at home there.

'London didn't agree with you.'

He shrugged and drank.

'Never could stand that place for long,' Sid said. 'The missus comes from there and we sometimes go back, just for the day. That's enough for me. The bloody prices they charge in those pubs! I dunno. It's all right for some.'

'That and the frigging traffic,' said the drinker at Wicks's elbow. 'Did you drive up, may I ask?'

'I drove up.'

'You wouldn't catch me! Not drunk nor sober.'

'He'd have the cops on his tail!' Sid winked. 'You can't go on burn-ups there, Jack.'

'Rotten filth,' Jack said. 'They did me here. And I was under the ton.'

Jack Stringer. An ageing biker. His cherished Speed Twin

19

was parked outside. Another lonesome type. Wicks saw his empty glass, nodded to Sid to refill it.

'Thanks,' Stringer said. 'My turn next. You have any trouble up there?'

'Just . . . the bloody jams.'

'Just the jams, he says! I mind me the last time I hit the Smoke . . .'

But Wicks didn't want to talk. He drained his glass, ordered another, refusing to let the biker pay. Then he bought a couple of cheese rolls from the covered dish on the counter and retired to a nook in the far corner of the bar. He sat, ate and drank. They were still talking about him, he knew. Now and then, one or another sent a look in his direction. So sod them . . . sod them all! Sod the gabbling bastards who sat around him. Was there one of them who could pull out a wallet like the one he felt weighing against his chest?

He finished the rolls, used the toilet, then sat down with another pint. The drink was beginning to do its work, to blur the edges of the image in his mind. It could have happened to any bugger, that! Any bugger at all. Just put them in the same position and they'd have acted the same way. Jack there in his leathers and his greasy hair. Sid the landlord, with his grinning face. Or one of these sods with their posh accents, their neighing laughs, their ceaseless chatter . . . Yes, anyone! Why blame himself? If it came to that, would anyone blame him? He could afford the best law in the country . . . they'd put it across for him. He'd surely get off . . . And for one wild moment . . . but then again! No. He felt for his glass.

'Fill me up!'

Sid stared. 'You're sure, now?'

'Yes – do you think I'm bloody drunk?'

'Well . . .' Sid shrugged, but reached for his glass.

And it happened again. The stupid bastard nearly didn't serve him, that time. What was he playing at? Wicks wasn't making trouble, was still on his feet . . . more or less! He staggered back to his corner and sat scowling. Five pints . . . six . . . what did it matter? No trouble. And he wasn't legless.

He should have told that bugger off . . . Why were they staring at him like that, as though he had just pissed on the floor?

He'd got another man in tow now, Sid, a big fellow who Wicks hadn't seen there before. He was staring too, and saying something – who did the bugger think he was? A bloke in a snazzy tweed jacket, with a pipe in his stupid mouth – square chops and smiling bloody eyes, with a tiddly glass of Scotch in his hand. And Sid, he was treating him like Lord Muck, or as though he too had a fat wallet . . .

Wicks hauled himself up. His sodding glass went sideways – wouldn't that have to happen just then? He kicked it under the table, straightened himself, lurched across the bar.

'A . . . Scotch like that!'

'Now Kenny, really – '

'A bloody Scotch . . . one like his!'

'Kenny, old boy – '

'A bloody Scotch! If he can have one, why can't I?'

'Kenny . . .'

'A bloody Scotch!'

Now the gabble had stopped. Everything had stopped. The eyes of the whole bar were on him. He was standing there before a counter that wobbled, scowling at a Sid who wouldn't stay still.

Then Lord Muck took his pipe from his mouth. 'Time you were leaving, laddie,' he said softly. 'There's always tomorrow.'

'But I want that Scotch . . .!'

'Come back tomorrow. You'll find it will taste better then.'

'But . . . I want it now!'

'No. Tomorrow.'

'But – '

Smilingly, Lord Muck shook his head.

'He's right, Kenny boy!' Sid said. 'You come back tomorrow and have some then. Just now you need your kip. Look, there's Jack here will give you a hand.'

'I tell you . . .!'

'Jack, give him a hand out.'

21

'I was leaving anyway,' the biker said. 'Come you on, man.'

And before he knew how it happened, Wicks found himself out in the cool night air.

Jack was propping him up. He was saying: 'Do you think you can make it home, now?'

'I'm going back in there!'

'Oh no you aren't! Do you know who that bloke was who was talking to you?'

'I don't bloody care!'

'Well you'd better. He's a top sodding policeman from Scotland Yard. He's got a house down here he comes to, that big one up by The Walks. So you'd best keep your nose clean, man, when you see him propping up the bar.'

'I . . . don't believe it!'

'Then bust your luck. But I'm not hanging around here any longer.'

He heard the Speed Twin break into raucous life and racket away through the village. It faded. Then he heard laughter behind the lit windows of the bar. Go back in there . . .? Tell the frigger? If he only knew who he'd just had slung out! If only . . . But then he retched violently, leaned for a long time against the wall. And the next thing his feet were walking, walking towards the empty house. If only . . .! He lurched through the still-gaping door and collapsed on a settee.

2

'Didn't know if I should wake you, Mr Kenny, but I thought maybe you could use a cup of tea.'

He was back in his bed, or rather on it, since he hadn't succeeded in undressing. He hadn't pulled the curtains, either, and now the morning sun was dazzling him: he groaned and covered his eyes with his hand. He had a taste in his mouth like a cow-pat.

'Put it down . . .'

'Were you late in, Mr Kenny? When I came here the front door was wide open.'

'Yes, Vera . . . late in.'

'Well, it's a good thing the folk here are honest!'

'Just put it down . . .'

She placed the cup on the bedside cabinet beside him – did she have to be so bright and bloody cheerful? His head was thumping, his limbs ached, he wasn't ready for that sort of thing. Yet there she stood, grinning down at him, all neat and tidy in her flowered housecoat. With a great effort he heaved himself up on his elbow and reached a shaky hand towards the cup.

'Shall I be cooking you some breakfast then, Mr Kenny?'

Oh hell! 'No breakfast, Vera.'

'But you should have something, now. Perhaps I could get you a bowl of shredded wheat.'

'No . . . nothing. I'll think about it!'

'Perhaps after you've had your shower, Mr Kenny.'

'Yes . . . perhaps then, Vera.'

'I'll get on, then. I dare say you've got some washing.'

She bustled out. He tried a mouthful of tea . . . oh God, it tasted vile! But it was something to rinse his mouth with and he went on taking repugnant sips. So he'd got himself up to bed – but what was it that had happened down there in the hall, when he'd been stretched out on the little settee, with its mahogany arm hurting his head? Something . . . yes! Now he remembered. In the dark, a furtive rustling and grunting. And suddenly his hair was standing on his head – had that bugger come back from the forest to haunt him? He'd lain there transfixed. It was coming closer! He had to do something – had to! In the end he'd staggered up from the settee, lurched down the hall and found the light switch. And . . . what was it? A bloody hedgehog! It had crept in through the open door, was snouting this way and that, looking for beetles or some sodding thing. . . . The light disturbed it, and with a grunt or two more it had turned about and trotted out again. He sipped revolting tea. It had to be the drink! Yet that moment of fear had been real. Just for those few seconds he couldn't help it, had lain there paralysed by the memory. Desperately he gulped back the tea, set the cup clattering on its saucer. All that was yesterday. Now, was a new day. The thing to do now was to put it behind him . . .

He dragged himself off the bed and down the passage to the old-fashioned bathroom, where the bath stood stark on claw-feet and the black rubber floor tiles were lifting. Deliberately, he let the shower run cold. The bloody thing nearly killed him.

After all, he did manage some breakfast, and Vera had brought in the morning papers. Quickly he leafed through the local, including the column of stop-press. Nothing, of course. How could there be? It was less than twenty-four hours . . . But then the thought struck him that the police, in their cunning, might just be sitting on the news. It was possible . . . but, bloody no! He must get ideas like that out of his head.

His part was to act normal, to think normal, to carry on as though it had never happened. Not like last night: then he'd been a fool – though he didn't know a copper had got his eye on him. He sat staring at the paper for a while, but was startled by the ringing of the phone.

'You . . . take it, Vera!'

'It's for you, Mr Kenny. A man from the bank wants to speak to you.'

From the first, the bank had appointed an adviser to help him manage his mountain of wealth. He took the phone.

'Wicks here.'

'Ah, Mr Wicks. I'm glad I found you in. I wonder if you've had time to give a little thought to the portfolio we suggested? I don't like to press you, of course, but the sooner we finalize our plans the better.'

Had he given it any thought? Not lately, anyway! 'I . . . I'm still thinking it over.'

'Of course. But what I'd like to suggest, if you have the time, is that you call in here this morning. There are several things I would like to discuss with you and we need your signature to go ahead. Would that be possible?'

'I . . . all right, then!'

'Good. Can we expect you around half-ten?'

'I . . . yes. Half-ten.'

'Then I'll look forward to seeing you, Mr Wicks.'

He hung up, scowling. All the time they were badgering him to invest in this, that, the other – as though he needed to make more money, when he didn't know how to spend what he'd got! But he'd go, it was acting normal, the way he was expected to carry on. A millionaire sorting out his millions. How could he ever be connected . . .?

'I'm off into town, Vera. Dare say I'll be having lunch with mum.'

'That's all right, Mr Kenny. I haven't done the shopping yet.'

He went out to the Jag, which had sat all night unlocked and with the key left in her. In a village like Welbourne . . .!

He paused a moment to stare at the peaceful green sloping down to the duckpond . . . yes, it was a pleasant spot and just a couple of miles from the sea. Surely, some day, his mother could be persuaded to retire to such a haven as this? Rather surlily, he got in the car, set the smooth engine purring. There was that fellow from the Yard, he remembered: He hadn't known about him. But so what? He clearly wasn't a trouble-maker, probably wasn't here very often. And by the time they discovered . . . if ever . . . No, he wasn't going to worry about him! He smoothed the Jag away slowly, sensuously, let it glide by the green. At the top was the junction that led to the forest . . . unconsciously, he found himself easing the car. Should he? No reason not to! No reason to show he was avoiding the spot. It was a familiar diversion, across the heath, through the trees: a diversion he frequently made when driving in to Wolmering. So? But his hand avoided the indicator, his foot pressed again on the pedal. Why . . . why? Bloody why? But the Jag purred on along the road direct . . .

He held on to himself for a couple of miles, to the point where the route joined the A road. Then he let go. Eighty. Ninety. The sodding ton. And a bit more! Oh . . . it didn't last long. All too soon he was having to brake and turn off to Wolmering, leaving the poor bastards to toot their horns and a swathe of rubber where he hit the junction. But it soothed him, he felt the better for it. He let the Jag drift on the road into town. On the outskirts he passed the newsagent's where he'd bought that winning ticket, and he made a V-sign as he went by – Wicko was back: back in town: back in the place where he belonged! Casually, he swept right under the nose of some lesser traffic and slammed the Jag in a slot across from the old cinema. So!

'If you remember, Mr Wicks . . .'

The bank was at the other end of the narrow high street, a street jammed with parked cars down one side, its pavements overflowing with the August influx of visitors. A sombre building, it looked across market stalls to the front of the town's grandest hotel, a classic elaboration of tall windows, bows, a verandah and moulded stonework. As a kid, he'd gone in awe of the place – only toffs and the famous stayed there! Well, no longer. He'd have a meal there, bloody stop the night if he wanted . . . if it came to that, he could buy the place, write a frigging cheque there and then . . .

'We decided, I think, on the following. You preferred to hold a large sum in your access account. If I may say so, I think you will find that a smaller disposition will suit your purpose. But that we can leave open to discussion. The balance of your portfolio will be divided like this. The first forty per cent of the remaining capital will go into a core holding of dual growth bonds . . .'

And if he could buy the hotel, he could buy the tart who'd just swaggered in there off the street, waggling her bottom, swinging her bag, her high heels tapping on the pavement. Yes, he didn't have to stop at street girls! A bint like that was well within his reach. He could almost smell her scent, feel his hands sliding over those curves . . . So Joyce would swear and his mother raise Cain, but bloody hell! He wasn't a eunuch . . .

'The remaining ten per cent, Mr Wicks . . .'

A couple of hundred stuffed in her stocking?

'. . . we will invest in emerging markets, the Pacific rim, China and similar opportunities. Of course, these are higher-risk ventures and will call for continuous monitoring. But the stakes are high. One or two of these markets have bettered two hundred per cent growth per annum.'

Money, bloody money! He jerked himself alert. Didn't this silly bugger understand that he'd got more than he could spend in two lifetimes? 'So what have I got to do?'

'I have the paperwork here. If you would just go over these forms and give us signatures where I've marked . . .'

He scowled. 'This is on the up and up, is it?'

'Mr Wicks! I think you may trust us. Your money will go into a client account and the investments will be made in your name. At each step we will keep you informed and you will receive full statements at the beginning of each month. Is that satisfactory?'

He grunted. Probably! But how the hell was he to know what they were up to? One thing was sure: No sod was going to argue him into cutting back on his access account. Two million he'd stowed away there and that's where the bugger would stay. 'Give us those forms, then!'

'With regard to what I was saying earlier . . .'

'Just give us those bloody forms!'

The man shrugged his city-suited shoulders and passed the papers across the desk. Wicks didn't read them – what was the point? To him they wouldn't mean a sodding thing. He shuffled through them, found the places marked, scribbled at each of them his stupid signature. The adviser received them back and placed them carefully in a file. Then he summoned up a frosty smile and advanced his hand across the desk.

'Now, let me congratulate you, Mr Wicks! You have just taken decisions that will keep you a very rich man.'

But . . . if only the sod knew what hand he was shaking!

Down below, Wicks collected another wad at the counter: no sense in running short of all that dosh . . .

Outside he hesitated, staring at the doors through which the trendy bitch had swaggered. But somehow he wasn't in the mood to push his luck and they'd probably have slung him out anyway. No: he would have to plan it, find a way to ease up to such birds. No use just swanning in there with a handful. It would need to be more subtle than that. So. He wandered back down the street, pausing to stare in shop windows, trying to surprise something he might like to buy, or at least a present he could take to mum. The trouble was, she was too choosy! The last time he'd taken her a swish sun-hat, the sort of thing you saw them wearing at Ascot: but not, it seemed, in Pier Avenue. She couldn't wear that! What would people think? She wouldn't even try it on. And the same with a coat he'd bought her, a lizard-skin bag, some embroidered gloves . . . Well, bloody flowers, then! Even mum liked flowers. He crossed the street to Wolmering's flower shop, stood a long time frowning before it and in the end bought a pricey bouquet of roses. Something to go with it? Scent? But no, he'd be on dangerous ground there! Just the roses. He gripped them firmly and set off in the direction of Pier Avenue.

'How much did you fork out for these, then?'

Nothing, but nothing would ever change at Sea View bungalow. Always, when she opened the door, emerged that mingled smell of cooking and polish. In the hall-stand stood his father's stick and on one of the pegs hung his old, stained trilby: his presence was there, silent, smiling, behind the sturdy little figure with the bushy grey hair. Nine years . . .? Ten, nearly. He felt a surge of despair. No, she would never leave this place. He would have to forget that idea.

'Oh mum! What does it matter?'

She sniffed the roses. 'Perhaps not much to you. But there's some round here who would think different.'

'Then . . . bloody let them!'

'Don't swear, Kenny.'

'Well it makes me swear, how you carry on!'

'You know your father wouldn't have allowed it.'

'Mum, for Christ's sake – '

'There you go again.'

He bit his tongue. What was the sodding use? 'Look, let me put them in water for you! I reckon that green vase is just about right. Then we can stand them on the sideboard.'

He took the bouquet from her and hastened into the kitchen. In an atmosphere of stewing greens and roasting meat he filled a vase with water and arranged the flowers. She stood watching, calculating, with firm, grey-blue eyes.

'There . . . how's that, then?'

'I suppose . . .' Her shoulders moved. 'I suppose you're not such a bad boy, Kenny. Or you weren't before all this happened. You used to be a good boy to me.'

29

'Mum . . . nothing's changed!'

She shook her head.

'It hasn't, mum. Really! If you'd only let me . . . you know. We could have some wonderful times together.'

Still she shook her head. 'You're different, Kenny. Somehow this money has altered you. I thought at first you would soon get over it, settle down again and be yourself. Only you haven't. It keeps going on. This London business is only the latest.'

'I was just bored, mum!'

'Call it what you like, but you wouldn't have done it in the old days. And don't bother to lie to me about it, I know very well what you'd have got up to.'

'But it didn't mean anything.'

'Can you believe that?'

'Yes, I'm telling you – !'

Her head shook again. 'You've changed, son, you even lie to yourself. Don't think you can put it over on your old mum.' She sighed. 'And then there's poor Joyce. Can't you even begin to see what you've done to her? She's a good girl, Kenny, they don't come better. And now you're losing her. And who can blame her for that?'

'But mum, it isn't too late – '

'I'm afraid it is. I had a talk with her on Saturday. The poor girl was in tears. She asked where you were and I had to admit I couldn't tell her. Still wearing your ring, she was. She kept twisting it all the time we were talking.'

'Mum, I'll make it up to her – '

'One day you'll learn there are things you can never make up.'

'But I can try!'

'It won't do any good, son. She knows you aren't the man she gave her word to.'

'But – !'

Her eyes jerked to the stove. 'Oh my goodness – talking to you!' She hastened to it, turned the gas down and snatched a saucepan from one of the rings. 'Look – if you want to make yourself useful, start setting the table in there. You're staying to lunch, I suppose? It's a good job I got a joint for today.'

Dully he picked up the vase, went through to the dining-room and began setting the table. He didn't have to think which drawer to go to, where the cloth was kept, the place-mats, the cutlery. So many times . . .! As a kid he'd helped his sisters set that table, as a schoolboy, as a young man, as a weary worker come home from the brewery. Nothing had changed . . . and suddenly he was staring at the old armchair in the corner, seeing him there, his father, pipe in mouth, slippers. A pipe – like that bloody policeman! Why did he have to be reminded of that? And from that to . . . No, he wouldn't think of it: it just wasn't him back there in the forest!

'We'll have the glasses out, Kenny . . .'

'Right you are, mum.'

'And bring me a couple of dinner-plates through.'

This was what was real, the smell of greens, the joint of pork that mum was forking on a dish. It reached back, it enveloped him, the smell of food in their kitchen: at that moment the rest was a dream, a stupid nightmare existing elsewhere.

'Are you going to carve for me?'

Did she need to ask? Ever since they'd lost dad he had performed this office. Now, automatically, he reached for the carvers and began to slice through her perfect crackling. She watched critically, frowning at the meat, then taking each plate and adding the vegetables. Gravy was trailed over all, and finally a spoonful of apple sauce.

'You can be such a good boy, Kenny, when you like . . .'

'Never mind that, mum! Let's eat.'

'But I can't help thinking. Perhaps it isn't too late, if only you could put all this silliness behind you.'

'Oh, mum! I'm really going to try. I will, and that's a promise.'

'If only I could believe that.'

'You can, mum. That trip to London was my last fling.'

'But . . . what are you going to do, Kenny?'

31

'I don't know. But I'll find something, I promise you that.'

She sighed and began to eat her pork. And of course, she'd put her finger plumb on it. What could he do? To take a job would be absurd, yet not to take one left him facing this blank. Could he run something, buy a business? But all he knew about was heaving barrels! No, it must be something else. Something . . . He set to and ate his pork.

'If you see Gwen at any time . . .'

He'd stayed to give a hand with the washing-up. Then he'd stuck some notes in the housekeeping tin – he knew better than to hand them to her. He kissed her and went. Went strolling up the Front. Something . . . something it had to be! Staring at the sea, he pushed past the visitors, walked on up the Front, heeding no one. Did it matter what? Any job at all! Yet he knew in his guts he would never seek one, never again clock in, clock out with that money pressing against his chest . . . Then? He stared out to sea, saw a long-shore boat heading for the harbour. Perhaps, if he bought one of those? But at once he was shaking his head again. It was no good, no bloody good: that frigging money had got him marooned. It was chains, it was a prison, it isolated him, set him apart . . . He might as well jump in the bloody sea and get it over, why not?

'Wicko mate – where have you been hiding?'

He glared at the man, a former workmate. Just for an instant, he could feel his fingers twitching, then he brushed past the fellow and strode on. Could it – could it happen again? Was he truly going round the bend? Blindly he turned into the town, past the market stalls, the frigging bank. When he came to where the Jag was parked he found a ticket tucked under its wiper. He pulled it out, tore it up and threw the pieces in someone's garden.

He reached the A road, unleashed the Jag, drove anywhere, he couldn't care less. But of course a lousy police car flagged him down – perhaps he was wanting the bastards to! Did he know he'd been touching eighty? They gave him the test, but that was under, bent his ear, wrote him a ticket, watched frowning as he drove away. The soft sods! Further on he hit the ton, just for a moment, and after that cut his speed to forty and watched a queue build up behind him . . .

But it was senseless. In the end he turned off into a by-road, let the Jag drift along narrow lanes, past farm entries, cottages, a ruined church. He didn't want to think. It was too late. All he could do was go on driving. This way he could lose himself, lose the Jag, perhaps deaden the memory of the last twenty-four hours. If it had happened it wasn't to him, to Kenny, Wicko, Gwen's brother . . . How could it be him? He just wasn't that sort! No . . . never. Forget it. Forget.

In a sort of trance he went on driving till at last he found himself approaching a town, and then he came to himself with a start. What the bloody hell was he doing here? He took the first opportunity to turn, pointed the Jag back towards Welbourne. He was feeling calmer, less on edge, those country miles must have taken effect. Now he was driving sensibly, holding the Jag at a steady fifty-five, even letting the mugs go past him – why bloody not? He had nothing to prove . . .

Vera had left him a plate of salad in the fridge along with a beef-patty and a bowl of trifle. With his new-found calmness he took them into the lounge, switched on the TV and sat down to eat. The local news was being shown. It didn't bother him – why should it? As bored as any other viewer he watched the trivialities of local happenings. Mum would be watching it back in Sea View, Gwen the early *habitués* of the Bell. Vera, across in her cottage. And he . . . how was it different with him? Almost, he didn't care! An item featured the forest and he found himself watching it with scarcely a qualm. No, he didn't care! He had got himself back again – he was Kenny, Wicko, and bugger all that . . .

The mood stayed with him. He put his crocks in the sink and set out down the green to the Bell. The lowered sun was casting shadows from the trees surrounding the pond. A few cars were parked there and the ducks were squabbling:

someone had just thrown them crusts of bread. On the green, a few strollers: by a gate, a couple gossiping. He strolled leisuredly, comfortably, Wicko on his way to the pub ... then he pushed through the door to find Lord Muck propping up the bar.

'Are you ready for that Scotch, now?'

'Just ... a pint, Sid.'

Why was that sod so interested in him? Because there was no doubt that he was: he was smiling at Wicks with those placid, green-hazel eyes of his. His pipe was going and, this evening, he too had a pint tankard on the counter beside him. There was something knowledgeable about that smile, as though the bloke had known you all your life. Had he met him some place before? Sid was grinning too as he pulled the pint.

'You haven't met the Chief Super before?'

'Well ... no. That's to say ...!'

Sid gave him a wink. 'I told him about you – how you had your little bit of luck!'

Wicks didn't know what to say. Nervously, he took a pull at his glass.

'I'd better introduce myself,' the man said. 'The name is Gently, but you can call me George. And you're Mr Wicks, I'm told, and someone rather special round here.'

'Well ... if Sid's told you ...'

The man nodded. 'Though I dare say you don't like having it spread around! But of course, it makes people curious, makes them wonder what they'd do in your position. At first, it must be quite a shock.'

'Yes ... well ...'

'I believe you used to work at a brewery.'

'Yes ...' Wicks took a pull.

'And now you could buy it! Though I don't suppose you would fancy that.'

What the hell was he getting at? Sid kept grinning in that

34

stupid way of his. Luckily there were only a few customers yet, and they were sitting at a table out of earshot. Wicks kept drinking. The man puffed on his pipe. Gently ... hadn't he heard that name mentioned somewhere?

'Are you married, Mr Wicks?'

'I ... no.'

'I expect you're still trying to come to terms with it all.'

'Yes ... it's like that.'

The man nodded. 'It can't have been an easy time for you, I imagine. Something like that changes everything from one day to the next, and at first you must have felt at a loss as to how you could handle such a windfall. I expect you'd be offered advice?'

'Yes, advice ... the bank.'

'But I daresay that's only the beginning.'

'The beginning ... yes.'

'Then you would have to work out where you were going after that.'

Wicks could only drink. This bloody bloke! It almost seemed he could read his frigging mind. Perhaps the sod could. Perhaps that's what it took to be a big noise in Scotland Yard. So ... let him carry on! One thing he didn't know, and the odds were he never bloody would.

'By now, I expect you probably have some idea. What you're going to do when it's all settled down. I don't envy you. It can't be simple. You must feel yourself under a great deal of pressure.'

Sod him, sod him. 'I'm ... still thinking! There isn't any hurry, is there?'

The man shook his head, and drank. 'I'm glad the problem isn't mine! I think I would need to stick to my profession for a bit, just to keep my feet on the ground. But you're a younger man, of course. And now the world is open to you.'

'Well, I don't want to buy their sodding brewery!'

The man chuckled. 'But something else?'

'Yes ... maybe! I don't know. But no so-and-so is going to rush me into it.'

35

The man's stare was solemn for a moment. Then he shrugged and drained his glass. He said: 'So it's been interesting meeting you, Mr Wicks, but now I must get along. I hope you don't think I have been too curious, only one doesn't meet such people as yourself every day.'

Wicks stared back but said nothing. The man gave Sid a wave and left.

Sid came to collect the empty glass. He gave Wicks a quick look. 'You didn't have to be like that. Kenny . . .'

'Just fill my sodding glass again!'

'He isn't a nobody, that bloke – '

'I've had enough. Just fill me up!'

But it was no good, his mood had been destroyed by that nosy bastard, he was back again glaring at the sea, blasting the road, hearing the siren. Could it really be that the bloke suspected something, could read it in his face? He wouldn't have put it past him to have made enquiries, to have learned of Wicks's binge and his night in the cells. The sod, the sod! And now he came smiling, pretending to understand . . .

No, it was no good. He took his beer to a corner, sat sipping and scowling at the glass. He didn't even feel like tying one on, that's what the bugger had done to him. And his mum . . . all of them. Rotten Joyce. Was there no one he could go to? Gwen . . . ? He shook his head: there was no bugger.

'Wicko . . . do you feel like some business?'

It was growing dark when he left the pub. Outside, this tart had sidled up to him . . . what was her stupid name? Sandra. Well . . . perhaps he did! Perhaps that was what he needed. Perhaps it was all he was bloody left with.

'You're on.'

She clung to his arm, leaned against him. He could smell her scent. She wasn't a bad girl, Sandra, she knew how to give value for money. He took her to the Jag in the drive. Then and there. Afterwards she nestled up to him for a while, warm, giving, tender. He stroked her hair. Suppose . . . ?

'What would you say if I told you I'd done something really bad?'

36

She giggled. 'What sort of thing?'

'I don't know . . . like killing a bloke?'

'Go on, Wicko!'

'But . . . if I had?'

'You're winding me up, and you know it!'

'But if it was true?'

She giggled again and snuggled closer. 'You're an old silly!'

'Wouldn't you believe me?'

'If you wanted me to. If it was giving you a kick.'

'No . . . but really.'

'Pull the other one, Wicko. In this game you hear it all the time.'

He offered to pay her with a couple of fifties, but she turned them down: too difficult to change. He had to count her out tens. She stuffed them in her bag, then gave him a kiss as though she really meant it.

'I'm going for a drink, now. Are you coming?'

He shook his head, remaining sitting in the Jaguar.

'Well . . . see you, old Wicko!'

'See you.'

It might have been an hour later when he locked up the car.

3

Surprisingly, he slept well – could Sandra have had something to do with it? – and woke with an odd feeling that a great space of time was lying between himself and the torments of yesterday. Below, a blackbird was tolling its alarm notes, early sun was shining on his curtains, while from across the green came the clink of bottles as the milkman delivered at one of the cottages. Yes ... suddenly, it seemed very far away, a dream, a memory from a distant year. what a stupid fool he'd been! But now it was gone, behind him, over. He stretched himself luxuriously and sat up, revelling in the innocence of the morning sun. He drew the curtains. The green sparkled with dew. On the bonnet of the Jag a black cat sat washing itself ...

'Your usual, Mr Kenny?'

'My usual.'

While it was getting he strolled out in the garden, the garden that had been let go since the old lady died, a whole year ago. Something he would have to do about that. His mum was most particular about her garden. Dad had kept it in applepie order, and ever since she had striven to maintain its perfection. When he'd lived at home he had mown the lawn for her and dug the plot for the vegetables – she had a man to do it now; but gardening wasn't an amusement of his. And here he wouldn't know where to start ... the rotten place went on for ever! Lawns, shrubberies, a greenhouse, sheds, and further on still some sort of a maze. And all of it a jungle, bushy, ruinous, rotting timbers, broken glass ... It would need professionals, a gang of them: just like the sodding house. Perhaps mum was right. Perhaps he should sell it, go in for a modern place, something more manageable . . .

Across the green, on a rising slope, they had recently built two or three executive-class houses: he strolled back to the gate to stare at them, at their state-of-the-art windows, their double garages . . . yes! That's what he should have gone in for, not this mouldering old ruin. Well, it wasn't too late. Not for him. He could buy those sods out twice before breakfast . . .

'Coo-ee, Mr Kenny!'

'Coming, Vera!'

His porridge was waiting, with the paper beside it. He ignored the latter, ate the former, accepted the plate of bacon-and-egg that followed. Having served him, Vera poured herself a cup of tea and settled herself in a corner of the kitchen.

'They tell me you've met our celebrity, Mr Kenny!'

'I've met . . . who?'

'Him up at Heatherings.'

'Oh . . . that one.'

Vera nodded smilingly. 'Said you had quite a chat with him, last night in the Bell. He's nice, isn't he? We all like him. His wife is French. Did they tell you?'

'No . . .'

'She's nice, too, and there's quite a tale about how they met. She got mixed up with a terrorist or something and he had to come to her rescue. Perhaps he'll tell you.'

He chewed his bacon. Did she have to rub his nose in this? Till that moment he'd forgotten the fellow, shoved him back in the nowhere where he belonged . . .

'Gabrielle, she's called. She's got a business in France. They must be quite well-to-do, him and her. I have a word with their housekeeper now and then, a Mrs Jarvis. She came from London with them.'

Shit on London! 'So what?'

'They've got a posh flat up there, too. Of course, that's

39

where he works, he's only down here weekends, and now and then when he gets time off. But I expect he told you.'

Wicks chewed savagely. Of course, the sod would have to be down here just now! Not that it mattered. He'd have to be a really lucky so-and-so if . . .

'They say he's a top man in his job, though it's not one everybody would want. He specializes in murder cases. It's a fact, Mrs Jarvis told me.'

'I don't want to know.'

'I'm not sure if I did! But there you are, someone has to do it. And he's as nice a man as you could want to know, you'd certainly never guess, just talking to him. Would you have guessed?'

'I . . . no.'

'There you are, it's like I say. And his wife, I expect she's used to it, though her being French perhaps it's different.'

'Vera . . .'

'Yes, Mr Kenny?'

'I . . . I'd like some more toast. And then I'm going to look at the paper!'

She started up. 'I'm sorry, Mr Kenny! And me yarning away here when there's work to do.'

She fetched the toast. He leafed through the paper. In the background he could hear the vacuum-cleaner moaning. How was it possible? With her stupid gossiping she'd thrust him back, back, back . . . so the sod specialized in murder, did he? Knew all about bodies and what had happened to them. Well, first some bastard had to find that body and he'd done a good job in tucking it away! And . . . if they did find it . . . what then? How could they tell when the man died? How connect it with him, with anyone, or begin to guess what the motive had been? As near as sod it, a perfect crime . . . Lord Muck could chew it over as much as he liked! He might guess, but he could never prove. Wicko Wicks had been one too many for him. He finished the toast, emptied the pot, slung the newspaper aside.

'I'm off out, Vera!'

40

'Mr Kenny, about lunch – '

'Don't bother. I'll have it out.'

On the bonnet of the Jag the cat still sunned itself, and regarded his approach with admonishing eyes. It sat up and stretched as he unlocked the door, then resentfully climbed down, waved its tail and stalked away.

He filled up at the local garage and while he was there felt a sudden compulsion. Where did they say that bastard lived ... up by the Walks some place, wasn't it? At once he was visualizing the house, an old-fashioned place standing back from the road, all on its own, looking down on the heather slopes that swept along the valley. Yes ... he'd passed it often, never once guessing who might live there. So why not today? Just to show the sod! He might even wave as he went by ... He paid the attendant, belted in and pointed his bonnet towards The Walks.

The road was narrow, bending past cottages, coming quickly to gorsy heathland. He was letting the Jag drift in second and for some reason he could feel his heart pounding. But what the hell! He was doing nothing special, just using this road out of the village ... except, and suddenly he remembered it, this was also a road that could take him to the forest. Well, he wasn't going there, was he? No! Just driving by The Walks. And in any case, if he really wanted to ... he set his jaw tight and sauntered on.

One came on the house quite unexpectedly after climbing past a bank of gorse decked out with foxglove. At the summit, suddenly, a drive departed to the right and beyond appeared the roofs, the chimneys, the upper windows, still partly hidden by a screen of birches and by a wall of matching red brick. He let the Jaguar pause. Old-fashioned was right! The place must be older than his house in the village. On the roof blue pantiles, at each side gabled wings, and lattice windows, one or two of them pegged open. Older, yes ... but in much better order! In the gravel drive there was never a weed. And

41

he could see past the house to a perfect lawn, trim flower-beds, a sculptured beech hedge. Sod him, sod him! And a French tart for a wife ... He scowled his malevolence at the house down the drive. But then, at a window, a duster was being shaken and a face paused to stare at the Jaguar. Wicks drove on.

But not far. Down a slope, out of sight, was a bit of rough parking where a track began, a track that wandered through a valley of gorse that was one of the features of The Walks. Already another car was parked there. Wicks bumped the Jaguar in behind it – hell, that fellow didn't own the place! He got out, locked the door and stood a moment gazing back in the direction of the house. Perhaps ... from down the valley? He couldn't have said why, but for some reason he wanted to see more of the house. He set off. The valley dropped lower. Its gorse- and heather-clad sides completely closed in the prospect. They were jungle, unbroken, impenetrable, leaving only the track threading the floor of the valley. If it was privacy the sod was after ...! But he sweated on. And at last he did come to it: a steep little footpath, climbing up through the gorse, reaching for the summit of the slope. He scrambled up it. Yes ... a view! Across another deep declivity, above another gorse-jungled height ... And then he froze. Because he wasn't alone. A bloody man stood there. And a bloody woman.

'Our favourite ramble, Mr Wicks ... let me introduce you to my wife, Gabrielle.'

Something he had to stutter, but Christ knew what it was. And the grinning woman, she was all over him, gabbling away nineteen to the dozen.

'My husband is telling me, Mr Wicks ... you are having this big win in the lottery, yes? So much money! I do not know – if it happened to me, I think I go crazy! But now you are getting used to it, yes? Is not such a terrible thing after all?'

And bloody Lord Muck was grinning too, in that sodding

42

know-all way of his, as though he could see right through you, knew the furthermost thought in your head . . .

'You have bought that big old house, yes? Perhaps soon now you will marry? There is a lucky girl? I think so, hah? One who is to share so much good fortune?'

Why couldn't she stop? 'I . . . perhaps!'

'Aha. I am telling my husband! This you will be needing, a partner to share, a good girl who will help you to manage your affairs. So shall it be soon?'

Lord Muck shook his grinning head. 'You mustn't press him like this, my dear! I think Mr Wicks is still coming to grips with it all, he isn't quite ready to take big decisions.'

'Oh, but this one . . . yes, I am sure!'

'You must forgive my wife,' Lord Muck said. 'She is a romantic first and last. For her, your first duty will always be to marry.'

'George – do not give me away! But shall we not take Mr Wicks back to coffee?'

'If you wish, my dear.'

'So – then?'

He could have hit her. And hit him.

'You will stroll back with us – yes?'

'I'm sorry . . .'

'No? You have other affairs?'

'Yes . . . I . . .'

'Oh, but please!'

'I'm . . . sorry.'

'Some other day, perhaps.' Lord Muck grinned.

'Yes . . .'

'So.' She shook her head disappointedly.

They parted. He went back down the footpath. He was seething. He stumbled, he fell. Swearing every oath, he picked himself up and strode back up the valley to his car. The bastard, the bitch! They were both of them in it. Both of them trying to make him look small. Rubbing it in. He was a bloody nobody. Just a sodding toe-rag who'd had a bit of luck. So who were they to treat him like that? A lousy French bint and a high-up pig – and one who didn't know who he was dealing with or, hell, he would have treated him different! Almost raving, he got back in the Jag, belted up, sat a moment or two glaring. He was pointing the right way, so ... why shouldn't he? What was to bloody stop him, what? He turned the key, drove. Sod them all. Sod them. Sod them!

He wanted to drive fast but couldn't, because of the windings of the narrow road. On one hand it skirted The Walks, on the other a field crimson with poppies. Then it wriggled down among trees and bracken and bent sharply, awkwardly, on a gradient, so that all the time he was having to hold back, drive carefully, like an old woman. And slowly, slowly the anger died in him, began to be replaced with something else. Uneasily, he was beginning to feel that he might have let his guard down, to have revealed himself to that bloke. Yet, how could he have done? Only he knew ... Unless the bloke could really read his mind: could tell from long experience that he was looking at someone who ... But that was crazy! It didn't happen like that. First, there had to be something for him to go on. And all he'd got was that moment in the pub when Wicks had come near to breaking loose. Had that been it? He'd smelt something there? A look in Wicks's eyes of what had happened? No ... it was too far-fetched, he was bloody imagining things. He made an effort to drive it from his mind. But still it clung there as the trees drew nearer. First came the heath, the picnic pull-off, with parked cars and people in plenty. Then the first brush with the sodding trees, a church, the edge of Grimchurch village. For a moment, open fields, marsh, a glimpse of the coast and the sea ... and after that up, up into trees that enclosed him on every side.

This way he'd come, this way, this way. He could feel his jaw gripping very tight. Past the old site ruined by the hurricane. Round the bend. Into the straight ... And there were people about there, bugger them, parked cars, sodding kids! Kids who were playing some frigging game, there, right there, beside the tank. Why were they letting them – it could be bloody dangerous, in spite of the netting he'd pulled back over . . . Didn't they realize? Were they plain stupid? So nearly he was pulling in to warn them, tell them . . . but he didn't. He kept driving. He drove past the entry and on, on. Why had he gone there, why had he risked it? He had to get out, get away from that place. Sweat was running down into his eyes: he brushed it away. And drove. Drove.

When at last the panic subsided he was approaching the village of Eastbridge, and there something – was it another part of him? – flashed and turned the Jag towards Walderness. Had he really meant to do that? For a moment he didn't understand, stared frowningly at the Wolmer river that had come into view, glinting, below him. Why this way? Then the curtain fell. Of course, of course: Gwen! His sister, the youngest, the nearest one, she who would talk to him, who he could talk to.

Always it had been like that with Gwen. The two years between them scarcely counted. They'd been kids together at school, had always been close, stood by each other. And now he wanted her, needed her, needed the contact she provided. Flo, the eldest, was no good. She took after mum, was if anything stricter. And Liddy was a remote sort of person, seemed to live in another world. No: it was Gwen who drew him. Who understood. He drove a little faster. If only he could tell her . . . Almost, he felt as though he could.

Her house was a new one at the beginning of the village and in the drive stood the new Rover 100 which he had given her. He edged the Jaguar in after it till the two cars stood bumper to bumper. At once the door of the house opened and his sister stood smilingly watching him climb out – a good-looker, Gwen! Today she was wearing a sharp flowered two-piece, also a present. She took a step forward.

45

'Well! My millionaire brother. And I thought he'd forgotten me!'

'Go on, Gwen! Why should I do that?'

He gave her a hug and kissed her cheek. She pushed back, smiling up at him. She giggled.

'I've just had mum on the phone – you know! She told me you'd been in town, giving the tarts up there a treat. Well, that's mum. Have you been in town?'

'Just the one night. And I spent it in a cell.'

'You never! So what was it about?'

'Don't ask me. I was bloody legless.'

Gwen giggled some more. 'You are a devil, Kenny! One day you'll get in a proper scrape. Was there any come-back?'

'Just a right telling-off. And they slung me out of their sodding hotel.'

'I'll bet they did!'

'So that's me, Gweny. What have you been doing with yourself?'

Still chuckling, she drew him into the house and sat him down in the spacious lounge – so different it was from his one at home, with its faded furniture and moth-eaten hangings. Gwen's looked new, smelt new, was all round the latest thing. In one corner was a fitted bar and there she poured him a pint and herself a gin.

'You're staying to lunch?'

'If you'll have me.'

'I'm afraid I was only having cheese.'

Dick, her husband, of course, was away on his travels, taking orders for computer soft ware from his clients. Gwen had done all right for herself. She'd met Dick Adams when she'd worked for an estate agent.

'All right for you?'

'Why not?'

'I thought you might have lost your taste for such simple things!'

'Well . . . we could go out.'

46

She shook her head. 'I'd rather have you to myself. It's quite a time since we had a chat and somehow you look as though you need it.'

'How . . . how do you mean?'

'Oh, I don't know! As though you were a bit fed up about something – are you? You can tell me, you know. I wouldn't let it go any further. Was it what happened in town?'

'Well yes . . . a bit.'

'Something else?'

'Perhaps. Something.'

She stared at him, drank. 'Are you going to tell me, then?'

He gulped bitter. And suddenly he knew. He couldn't tell Gwen, couldn't tell anyone. Nobody else in the bloody world. He was stuck with it. It stayed with him.

'Is it Joyce who's bothering you?'

'Joyce . . . I don't know!'

'You've really been trying her patience, old Kenny.'

'Please! Let's not talk about it, shall we?'

'Well . . . if that's the way you feel.'

'I'm sorry, Gweny. But just now . . .'

Gwen finished her drink. 'You old silly!' She got up. I'll go and get our lunch,' she said. 'You're probably hungry. You stay here. There's the telly there if you want it.'

'No . . .'

'Or those magazines.'

She went. He sat on. He could hear her laying out plates and cutlery. The knuckles of the hands that gripped his glass were white. He stared at the glass, didn't drink. Nobody. Nobody. He could tell nobody. He was stuck with it for ever. Always, always it would set him apart. He had done the thing that could never be told. He almost screamed. Then who was he? Whose was the body sitting here? It wasn't him, wasn't Wicko, wasn't the kid brother of the woman out there. Then who? Who? Who? Who was sitting there, squeezing that glass? He bent over it, trying to crush it – at least, at least that would prove he was someone!

47

'Ken-ny!'

Did she know who she called? Ought he to respond and play that part?

'Kenny – it's ready!'

Mechanically he rose, still clutching the glass, which he'd only half-emptied.

'Shall I get you another one?'

'No . . . this will do me.'

'I've got the coffee perking for after. Now sit down and tuck in. Luckily, I did the celery earlier.'

He obeyed her mindlessly. She'd cut him a a thick slab of his favourite Jarslberg and served it along with a couple of fresh rolls, tomatoes, two sticks of celery. He buttered his rolls and ate. Kenny. Wicko. Gweny's kid brother. That was his role, and he had to play it, make it stick. Now. For ever.

'I got the cheese at Tesco. What do you think of it?'

'Nice . . . a bit of all right.'

'I like it too, but Dick prefers Stilton. Personally I've never been fond of that.'

'It tastes like chicken-muck.'

'That's what I say! But you can never argue with Dick.'

He ate on. Wasn't it possible to put that darkness behind him . . . to cut himself off from it, remember it only as something that had happened to someone else? Because it hadn't been him! Another person had taken over, he'd been possessed back there by someone, something. And now, bloody now . . . There must be a way, a way to get back . . .

'Do you mind having doughnuts for afters? They're fresh, I bought them this morning.'

'Okay with me.'

Her brown eyes stared at him. She munched on a piece of the celery. 'You don't have a lot to say for yourself, Kenny. There's something wrong with you, isn't there?'

'I . . . don't know!' He kept his eyes on his plate. 'Perhaps . . . well, every bloody thing!'

'It's Joyce, isn't it?'

'Joyce . . . Mum.'

'Oh, we know how mum carries on! She'll come round, she always does. You don't have to worry about mum. But Joyce, now she's different, Kenny. You must realize how she's feeling.'

'I know!'

'Well, it's up to you.'

'All right, all right!'

'I mean . . . she'll probably understand. It went to your head a bit, all this, and you had to have your little fling. But you've got to let her see it's over, that you're ready now to settle down. She isn't a fool. She'll understand. You've just got to make her feel you're through with it.'

'Oh . . . bloody hell!'

'It's your decision, Kenny. You must know you can't go on like this.

'I know, I know.'

'So there you are then. You'll feel a lot better when you've cooled things down.'

He tore a roll savagely and crammed some in his mouth, grabbed his glass, washed it down, finished the rest in two bites. It could have been rotten Flo sitting there, preaching to him what he had to do . . .

'You aren't happy, Kenny, are you?'

'Look, Gwen . . . it isn't so easy.'

She shook her head. 'It can't be. You never have seemed happy, ever since it happened. So what are you going to do?'

If only he knew that! 'I . . . I don't know. I'm going to try, Gweny. From now on, I'm going to try.'

'My advice is, make it up with Joyce. She's the one who'll get you back on the rails. You need her, Kenny. She's got her head screwed on. But you'll have to let her know you really mean it.'

'It isn't . . . just that.'

Her eyes were keen. 'You aren't in some trouble, are you, Kenny?'

49

'No! What I'm trying to say is . . . well, it isn't easy, the way things are. The money and all . . . I'm stuck with the bugger. I don't know which way to turn next.'

'You mean, what you want to do?'

'Yes. Like that.'

Gwen stared, then giggled. 'You poor old sod! Stuck with all that dough behind you. I wish it was me with that problem, Kenny.'

'You wouldn't if you had it.'

'Just try me!'

He scowled. 'So what would you do?'

She stared happily at the ceiling. 'First, I think I'd sod off to Paris, visit all the fashion shows and buy clothes till I dropped. Then I'd travel, I'd go to the South Seas, to Hollywood, New York. Then I'd come back and set Dick up in his own business, and – I don't know! Buy a villa in Cannes. Won't you lend me a few mill, bro?'

'No . . . but seriously?'

'I'm dead serious!'

'You wouldn't do any of these things, Gweny.'

'Just try me, that's all! And now I'd better fetch those doughnuts.'

He stared after her neat, well-dressed figure. Was it possible to carry on like that? Well, perhaps for Gweny! For him, he didn't know the ropes, wouldn't even know how to begin. A bloody yokel, that's what he was, stuck here in the place where he'd been brought up. That's how they'd seen him in frigging London, how Lord Muck and his wench saw him down here . . .

'Black or white?'

'Black . . .'

She placed his cup and doughnut before him.

'I've been thinking, Kenny. Why not have a real go at that funny old place of yours? Dick knows a few people. You could do up the house, modernize it, make it really something. Then you could get in a landscape gardener. You could make it the smartest place in Welbourne.

50

Could he? 'Yes, I suppose . . .'

'Mum would approve, I can tell you that. And Joyce . . . she would have to believe that you meant to turn over a new leaf. So what about it?'

'Yes, perhaps . . .'

'I'll talk to Dick about it tonight. One of his clients is an interior designer and I'm sure he'll know the right builder to go to.'

'It'll be a bit of a fag, Gweny . . .'

'Go on, it's what you need! It'll keep you out of trouble.'

He made a face over his coffee. But yes, he could feel himself warming to the project. Perhaps she was right: perhaps it was what he needed, something constructive, something looking ahead . . . He ate, drank.

'So what about it?'

'I . . . don't mind talking it over with Dick.'

'It could be the answer, poor old Kenny. You've been looking so fed up with life just lately.' She paused. 'Want me to have a word with Joyce?'

If she bloody had to! 'All right.'

'I'll just say you'd like to see her. You can tell her about the house yourself.'

She kissed him as he was leaving and in his mirror he could see her staring after the car. Something she'd noticed . . . it was always the same with her, she had always been able to see through him. Could he, should he have told her? The impossibility caught at his throat. No. Never. Never! And as much for her sake as his own. It was behind him, must stay behind, he must set his back to it and look forward. Forward in the direction she had suggested to him. The house. Joyce. Forward!

He barely noticed the turn when he made it or where the bonnet of the Jaguar was pointing. Just that a chill was rippling through his flesh and that, suddenly, the trees were around him. Why . . .? He sought to accelerate, but his foot refused to obey him. Slowly, like a visiting ghost, he slid past that hellish spot. One car only. The kids were gone. One car, with a couple standing by it. Not looking towards him. The bloke had binoculars, was gazing at a tree to which the woman was pointing. And the bloody Jag seemed almost to stand still, to hold that place in his vision for ever. Then, years later, his foot stabbed the pedal and the spectacle vanished as though it were a dream.

4

At breakfast, the phone rang.

'See to it, Vera!'

'It's your mum, Mr Kenny.'

He went through to the hall reluctantly: his head was still tender from the night before. When at last he'd gone down to the Bell he had pushed the door ajar cautiously, but it was all right, Lord Muck wasn't there, just Biker Jack and a handful of regulars. So he'd gone in and set them up – a Scotch or two amongst the rest – sitting up at the counter, nattering to Sid and that stupid sod in his greasy black leathers. And he'd told them. About the house. How he was going to turn it into a palace. And the snooty oldies had been cocking their ears, making comments to each other, sniggering. Well . . . let them! Let them all hear. When they'd seen what he was going to do with that place . . .

'Kenny?'

'Mum.'

'Listen, Kenny. You weren't on the drink last night, were you?'

'Oh, . . . Mum.'

'Well, you sound a bit like it. And I've got something serious to say to you.'

'I'm stone cold bloody sober!'

'If you say so. And please don't swear when you talk to me. Now. Joyce called in here first thing and asked me to speak to you. It seems she had Gwen on the phone last night and Gwen told her you would like to see her. I can tell you she wasn't too keen, but this is Thursday, her day off. So if you have anything sensible to say to her, she is willing to fit you in. Are you listening?'

Hell! 'Yes, I'm listening.'

'You do want to see her, don't you, Kenny?'

'Yes . . . I want to see her.'

'Then I'm glad to hear it, because this may be your last chance, son. Joyce has had enough and she won't wait for ever. It's good of her to let you see her at all.'

'Mum, please!'

'It isn't too late, Kenny. Not if you promise her you'll change your ways. That is why you want to see her, isn't it? To say you're sorry and that you want to try again?'

He closed his eyes. 'When am I to see her?'

'She says call round after half-past ten. You'll want to see her alone, of course, so she's willing to come out for a drive. Take her somewhere nice, son, and have a quiet little lunch somewhere. And be good to her, do. You know you have a lot to answer for.'

'Yes, yes. I'll do all that.'

'She's the one for you, son. And don't you forget it.'

Was he ever likely to, with mum on his back?

He hung up edgily. Things were going too fast! It had been all right yesterday, talking to Gwen . . . Then, last night, all that boasting in the pub . . . and now, before he could even catch his breath!

He went back to his breakfast. Yes, he wanted these things, felt, like Gwen, that this was the way: but not quite so suddenly. He needed time to get used to them, a breathing spell, a bit of a pause. They were going to change his life. He could see it now – this faded old house a designer's mansion, with Joyce ensconced here, running it, and later on . . . kids? For a moment he panicked! But that was how it would be, with Gwen, mum, everyone applauding. Could he stand for that, such a bloody future? Well . . . perhaps. But the sods should stop rushing him!

'I've got chops for lunch, Mr Kenny. I was down there early and got some beauties.'

'I'm afraid they'll have to wait, Vera.'

'You'll be out, will you?'

'Mum's orders, Vera.'

'Oh, Mr Kenny!'

He finished breakfast, glanced at his watch, went out for a stroll in the tangled grounds. The black cat had caught a bird, he saw, and went scuttling past him making raucous noises. A killer cat . . . he checked himself! He ought to keep his mind on this lousy garden, what in the hell they could do with it, how make it a frame for the new-minted house. He forced his way through overgrown shrubberies, past a dried-up pond, a collapsing summer-house. It was going to take for ever . . . and did he really want to sort it out? Perhaps he didn't. He rather liked it like that, a sodding jungle that went its own way, had its own forceful personality. Didn't it suit him, the way it was?

But Joyce, mum, Gwen – not to mention those sniggering sods in the pub . . . and Lord Muck, of bloody course! With his garden where not a blade was out of place . . .

Cut and run?

For a moment he felt like it, like jumping in the Jag and getting to hell. Clearing off to those places Gwen had talked about, wiping the whole bloody slate clean. He had the means, Christ he had the means. He could start off from scratch in some far-off place. And over there, on the other side of the world, would he ever need to look back over his shoulder . . .?

But the madness died. He couldn't do it. He didn't know how to frigging do it. To start with, he didn't have a passport, didn't even have a clue about how to get one. No. He was just a bloody yokel, an ignorant sod, a toe-rag who happened to have some money. No escape. Where he was he was stuck. Where he belonged. Sodding here!

He looked at his watch, turned about, began slowly thrusting his way back through the jungle. The black cat was back on the Jag again and, jumping off, left blood-stains and feathers on the bonnet.

'She'll be down in a moment, Kenny. Would you like me to make you a cup of tea?'

Always he felt like a kid again when he visited that house, one of a semi-detached pair that stood only yards from his mother's bungalow. In fact you could see the bungalow, its slate roof peering over the neighbours' hedges, and the Bramley apple tree, now crowded with fruit, which dad had planted at the bottom of their garden. In those days Joyce had been Gweny's pal, but he had always been welcome to tag along. The Clements had a swing – it still stood there – which had been a favourite plaything of his. And there had been one famous occasion when Joyce had said: 'Do you want to have a look?' Five, had he been? Six? Of course, he knew that his sisters . . .

'Don't bother, Mrs Clements.'

'It wouldn't be any trouble, you know!'

'I expect we'll be going out somewhere.'

'Well, you're very welcome, Kenny.'

A rather gaunt woman, taller than mum, and with her grey hair worn in a bun. He had the impression that his good fortune meant rather more to her than to her daughter. Her husband, a retired bus-driver, was doubtless out on his morning promenade.

'Do sit down while you're waiting – she can't be very long now! But you know what these girls are.'

'I'm all right, Mrs Clements.'

There was the smell of that house, too, a smell like apples but with a sharper edge. Was it the polish? From his youngest childhood he had noticed that smell, so different from the bungalow's. The Clements' smell. Joyce's. The smell that signified he was a stranger . . .

'Here she comes, now!'

Yes: and he could feel his muscles tensing. They had been

standing in the hall below the stairs and at the top of the stairs she had appeared. For a moment she paused, smoothing her frock, then came on down with little running steps. She gave the frock an added touch before facing him with forceful eyes.

'Gwen said you wanted to see me, Kenny.'

'Yes . . . I thought – '

'Well, here I am!'

'I thought . . . the car's outside . . .'

'Oh, we're going somewhere, are we?'

'Yes . . . well . . .'

'It better hadn't be the Ritz – I'm only dressed for a coffee-shop.'

Did she have to be like that, with her stupid mother standing by? No, she wasn't dressed for the Ritz – more like for another day at the supermarket! A beige frock with cream facings, that was good enough for Wicko, would put the lug in his place. Because who did the sod think he was?

'What exactly did you have in mind, then?'

'I thought . . . perhaps a run out Harford way . . .'

'As far as that?'

'Well . . . whatever you want! And a bite of lunch, you choose where . . .'

She stared at him. Considered him. And suddenly he was aware of the colour of her eyes – green-hazel, like Lord Muck's! Why had he never noticed their colour before? She gave her head a chuck.

'Very well, my man! If that's what you have in mind. But you must promise me we won't be late back, because I've things to do for tomorrow. Understood?'

'Yes . . . of course!'

'Then we'd best get on our way. Expect me back about tea-time, Ma, if you don't see me before.'

'Have a nice time, Joycey!'

'I'll try.'

She headed Wicks to the door. Mrs Clements laid her hand on his arm. 'Be nice to her, Kenny,' she said. 'Be nice!'

Had she noticed that Joyce wasn't wearing her ring? She stood a moment at the door, watching them get in the car.

'For the moment, just drive!'

It was the first time Joyce had been in the Jag. She herself drove a middle-aged Fiesta and she had scorned his offer to replace it. Now she belted herself in meanly and sat staring over the Jag's ranging bonnet, hands gripping her small bag, a sullen expression on her comely face. Was there any point in what he was doing? He adjusted his belt, set the engine purring. The last person to sit in that seat had been the tart, Sandra . . . another omen to add to the absence of the ring! He drove, as bidden, along the Front. Where they passed couples strolling, arm in arm.

'Harford way . . .?'

'Where you like.'

He wriggled the Jag back into the town, down the cluttered high street, past the lottery-ticket shop, over the little bridge: into the country. Oh yes, he was driving with care! There'd be no bloody ton on the cards today. Softly, silently he let the Jag glide: as though he'd got mum sitting there beside him. He hit the A road. He was barely doing fifty. He could see the queue begin to build up behind him . . .

'Oh, don't mind me!'

'I thought – '

'Just get on, if you don't mind.'

'Well . . .'

He let the Jag drift at sixty, perhaps a shade more – in the Jag you scarely noticed. And still she sat determinedly staring ahead, hands tight on the little bag. Would she ever loosen up? Perhaps some music . . .? He glanced at the stereo, but made no move.

'I just don't know why Gwen thought it might help!'

Now she was staring down at her hands. He stayed silent. At least she was talking! Best to let her get it off her chest . . .

'It took this rotten money to show me what you were.

Before that I really looked up to you, Kenny. You worked hard, you were good at your job, you were certainly in line for promotion. I felt sure of you. I'd known you so long. From the time we were kids we seemed meant for each other. And then . . . this happened! And suddenly I didn't know you, you were a stranger, a right nasty piece of work. I don't like saying that, Kenny, but it's true. And I could never, ever trust you again.'

Still he bit his lip and hung on. They were approaching the junction for the village. Should he take it . . .? Better not! Best to keep clear while this was going on . . .

'Have you nothing at all to say to me? I suppose Gwen told you it was worth a try! Well, now you know it isn't. My mind is made up. I've done with you, Kenny. This silliness with your money I could perhaps understand, it was enough to turn anyone's head. Together, perhaps, we could have sorted it out and kept you from going completely overboard. But that's not all, is it? There's scarcely a skirt you haven't chased. And now you're spending weekends in London and everyone knows what you're up to there. From the start you haven't given me a thought, Kenny, and I've made my decision. We're through!'

'Joyce . . . please!'

'No. Kenny. No.'

'It isn't how you think!'

'I said no.'

'But if only . . .'

She shook her head at the bonnet and went on shaking it.

Was it worth carrying on? He drove scowlingly, barely noticing where they were going, what speed they were driving at. It was stupid Gwen who'd let him in for this! Well, that was over, and all the rest of it, the bloody house, the stinking garden. There was no sense in going on with that, it was all of a piece. He was finished with it. He drove, drove, eyes fixed ahead . . . and then suddenly realized that she was crying! Crying, snivelling, tears rolling down her cheeks – what the hell was up with her now? He took the next junction off the A

59

road, found a verge under trees, parked the Jag. What to do next?

'Here ...'

He pulled the smart handkerchief from his jacket pocket. She took it, dabbed, wiped, snivelled into it afresh.

'You've been rotten to me, Kenny, rotten!'

'Look – !'

'What's the use of saying anything? You didn't care! After all we'd planned, all we'd dreamed. You just dropped me!'

'Joycey, it isn't like that!'

'Don't lie to me, Kenny! You dropped me. As soon as that money was in your pocket I was somebody in your past.'

'No!'

'Yes. Do you think I was blind?'

'Joycey, I tried!'

'Yes – you tried!' She scrubbed at her eyes. 'You tried to bribe me, that's what you did, as though I were some little tart from the streets. I could be bought. You could pay me off. It was just a question of how much money! You simply didn't realize how insulting it was to me, how degraded you were making me feel.'

'Please, Joyce, please!'

'You're a louse, Kenneth Wicks!'

'I didn't mean it like that – I just wanted to share it!'

'Yes, while you had other women from here to breakfast!'

'I just wanted to share – '

'Tell that to your tarts!'

She screwed the handkerchief up and threw it at him, then jerked her head aside and stared at the fields.

For a long time he did the same. He couldn't think of anything to say or do. He knew she'd had it in for him, but not like this! She wasn't giving him a chance to get back together with her. What was it she'd called him ...? A right nasty piece of work! And she had meant it, she'd bloody meant it ... Helplessly, he stared at the field of ripe wheat, at a combine he could see in the distance.

'Are we going to be stuck here all day?'

For a moment, his body wouldn't obey him. Then his hand twisted the key, an engine awoke, the car they were sitting in bumped off the verge. Where was it going? A road began to unfold. Maybe it led somewhere, maybe not . . .

'I'm thirsty. Would it be too much to ask you to stop here for a drink?'

Vaguely, he remembered the village, though he could by no means put a name to it: a straggle of anonymous houses, a sail-less smock-mill, and a pub. The latter had parking. He turned the Jag on to it, drifted it into a patch of shade.

'Are you coming?'

He'd let her get out before he reached to release his belt, and even then had sat a moment. But in the end he followed her into the pub.

'A half of dry cider for me.'

'A pint of Webster's.'

They took their drinks to a picnic table outside. She drank. He drank. They stared round at the garden, a weeping willow, the smock-mill. Finally her eyes met his for a brief instant. She drank some more, rested her glass.

'Do you know what you're going to do now?'

'Gwen . . .'

'Well?'

'She didn't tell you?'

She gave her head a little snatch. 'All Gwen told me was that you wanted to see me!'

'But . . . about the house?'

'What about it?'

He drank. 'I'm going to do it up. A proper job. She's talking to Dick. We're going to get an expert on it.'

'Really?'

'The garden too. One of those landscape-designer blokes. And all that furniture, that's coming out. It'll all be new, from top to bottom.'

'And this is what you wanted to tell me?'

61

'Yes.' He nodded.

She drank and stared at the smock-mill. A couple of pigeons had dropped down beside them, ran back and forth cooing, pecking at the pavement.

'Don't you . . . think it's a good idea?'

'Oh yes. A very good idea.'

'I thought perhaps . . . well, you know!'

She sighed. 'Yes. But it's a little too late.'

'But . . . Joycey!'

'I'm sorry, Kenny.'

'If . . . I promised you . . .?'

She shook her head and drank up. 'Let's go.'

He had to leave half his pint, but he followed her to the car. Well, perhaps she was right, and it was too late . . . too late ever since . . . He backed out, turned, set the Jag rolling, rolling he didn't give a damn where. Too late. And bloody Gwen had rushed him into it. Couldn't he have told her it would come to nothing?

'Turn here. We can lunch at Thwaite.'

Blindly he accepted her instruction. And yet, and yet . . . if she could only forgive him. Was it too much to expect her to understand? So he'd kicked over, it had gone to his head, he had treated her badly, oh yes! But bloody hell, it would have happened to anyone, why expect him to behave like a plaster saint? And now . . . now, yes, he meant it! He was ready to draw in his horns, to calm down, pick up his life again. He was ready. He'd shot his bolt . . .

'Did you really want to talk to me, Kenny?'

He clung tight to the wheel. 'Yes!'

'It wasn't just Gwen's idea?'

'No . . . she knew I wanted . . .'

'She was just trying to help.'

'I suppose so!'

'You convinced her you were ready to start over.'

He hung on, drove, kept his gaze on the road ahead. She was looking at him, he could feel it, those firm eyes were watching his face.

'Well?'

'You know I am!'

'No, I don't know that, Kenny.'

'But it's true!'

'I only have your word for it and you've broken it too many times in the past. How am I to trust you?'

'Because . . . this time . . .'

'You will have to prove it to me, Kenny.'

'I will, I promise . . .'

'No more wild goings-on, no women. No nights in police cells.'

'Gwen . . . told you that?'

'Gwen told me. She thought that at last it had shaken some sense into you. Has it, Kenny?'

'She shouldn't have told you.'

'She thought I should know. And she was right.'

He'd been letting the speed rise and now he hit a bend much too fast. Suddenly her hand had found his knee, just as it would in the old days. He eased off. The hand rested there a moment, firm, warm, reassuring, then was withdrawn. He saw it close again on the little bag.

'Weren't you going to tell me?'

'Perhaps . . . if you'd ever let me get round to it!'

'I wonder.'

'Why do you say that?'

She sighed and shook her head.

But she was thawing, he could sense it, had felt it in the hand pressed to his knee. She was coming round. There was a chance yet. He hadn't quite thrown it all away. Now he looked at her, a quick glance, and caught almost a glint of amusement in her eye. Yes, it was bloody on! Gwen hadn't been such an arse after all.

'Watch your driving, do.'

'What do you think of the car?'

'Never mind the car! Watch your driving, you've always been too casual about that.'

He watched his driving, said no more. Shortly they were

gliding into Thwaite.

'The pub on the corner.'

It was serving lobster salad and he confined himself to a single half of bitter.

Over lunch they'd talked family matters, almost as they used to before the rift happened, but when they came out she was silent again, and stood a while by the car, surveying the scene. Then she said: 'Let's drive to the Cliff. It's too early to go home yet. We could take a stroll by the river – we haven't been that way in years.'

The Cliff was a high, sloping meadow with a sweeping prospect of the marshes and the river. About a mile distant from the village, it was a dedicated picnic area and park. Today it was busy. He parked briefly at the summit, then idled the Jag down to parking below; from there, a track departed along the muddy margins of the tidal stream. They got out and he locked the car. Silently, she led the way to the track. They weren't alone. Ahead, little groups of visitors dotted the shore-line. The path wound vaguely between reedy mud-flats and the trees of the descending ridge, on the nearer slopes of which a house or two peered down. It passed an old boat-house and a few stranded boats, then emerged from the shadow of the trees. As they progressed, the visitors grew fewer. They came to an old yacht, half buried in mud.

'Let's sit for a bit.'

She found a seat on the tilted deck of the yacht and he shored himself up beside her, his feet almost in the mud. Here the river wound about low, reeded islands where wading birds pondered and ducks swam against the tide. She watched the birds. Then she opened her bag and took from it the ring she was no longer wearing. She gazed at it.

She said: 'You'll have to show me you mean it, Kenny.'

He kicked at the mud. A couple of black-and-white birds flew by, hooting.

'Do you think you can do it?'

'Yes – all right, then!'

'I won't accept any less, you know. I want a man, a decent man. Not a rotten sod who doesn't respect me.'

He splattered mud. 'I said all right! I know – I know I've let you down. I've been a fool, a bloody fool. But it's going to alter now.'

'I've got to be sure of that.'

'Yes, I know!'

'Marrying someone is a big thing.'

'You've got to give me a chance, Joycey!'

'After this, I won't listen to any more excuses.'

He kicked mud. She fingered the ring. Just then two visitors went by. They smiled at the pair sitting on the old yacht and the man stooped to pick up some object.

'Of course, I'm trying to understand. I can see how what happened might knock someone off balance. But even allowing for that, Kenny. I thought you had enough backbone to take it in your stride.'

'I know. I bloody know.'

'You must see how it makes me feel about you.'

'Yes – yes!'

'I can't take any chances, Kenny. You've got to prove you're still the man I once took you for.'

He wriggled on his comfortless seat. 'Joycey, listen!'

'I'm listening, Kenny.'

'Well – look! I really do mean this. I really want us to get back where we were before. I've had enough. I've been a fool. You just don't know what it's like till it hits you. But it's over now, all over.' He belted mud. 'I'm asking you to forgive me, Joycey.'

The ring was trembling. 'But . . . how can I be sure?'

'You can, you can. I'll do any bloody thing. The house, it's for you I'm getting it ready. And anything else! You've only to tell me.'

'I just . . . don't know!'

'You do, Joycey!'

He grabbed her, tried to kiss her. But she thrust him away.

'No – not yet!'

'Please . . . Joycey!'

But she turned her back, crushed the ring in her palm.

'I need time – I'll have to think about it!'

'But Joycey girl – !'

She shook her head. 'It's no use, Kenny. You've hurt me too much. I think it's time we went back to the car.'

'But we can't leave it like this, Joycey!'

'I'm afraid we'll have to. And stop making a fuss. Some people are coming this way.'

She jumped to her feet and began walking. For an instant he sat rigid on the side of the yacht. Nearly, so bloody nearly! Almost that ring had been back on her finger . . . He jumped up too and ran after her. But she walked on determinedly, her face averted. And a load of bloody people were advancing towards them . . .

At the car she surveyed him with a long stare, then held out her hand, the ring still in it. 'For the moment, you had better keep this!'

'For the moment . . .?'

'Until we know where we stand.'

'But . . .!'

She shook her head. 'I'm sorry, Kenny! We'll just have to see how things work out. Perhaps you really are a reformed character, and I'm ready to have you prove it to me. But I have to be certain. Until then, I think you had better keep the ring.'

'Joycey!'

'No, Kenny. Take it.'

And it was pressed in his hand, still warm from her own.

He drove back fast. She didn't complain. All he wanted now was to get rid of her. He dropped her at her gate and she didn't ask him in. He aimed the Jag straight back towards Welbourne.

So he was on probation now, was he – on his honour to live like a saint! No booze-ups, no business with Sandra, with high-heeled little tarts like the one in Wolmering. From now on, a sodding hermit, alone in that mouldering house, visiting mum, visiting Gwen, his meals got by crinkle-faced Vera. Was it worth it? But he had to pause there! Because yes, deep down, he knew this was what he wanted: a way, a way forward. The way his stupid sister had suggested. At whatever bloody cost . . . And bloody cost him it was going to!

'Would you like those chops now, Mr Kenny?'

Somehow, he would have to make it stick, somehow forget his lousy money, get back to the style of all those others. If only . . . But bloody hell! He had put that behind him, hadn't he?

When Vera went he fetched cans from the larder, switched on the TV and sat down to stare at it. A long while after, the screen had gone blank and he couldn't find a sodding can with a drop left in it.

5

The next day he rang Gwen, but Gwen wasn't in and he hadn't the heart to ring the bungalow. Joyce was back at work, of course, and couldn't be reached until the evening. He sat frowning at the phone, his head still thick. Vera hadn't roused him till mid-morning. Then all he could manage was a bowl of cornflakes and a gallon of strong tea.

He felt baffled: what had really happened yesterday? He didn't seem able to get a grip on it. Was he back with Joyce, or wasn't he? – he couldn't get the situation straight in his mind. First she had let him have it properly, calling him a nasty piece of work, telling him that she was through with him and that she could never trust him again. But then she'd cried – he'd never known her to cry before! – and then she'd softened up and let him talk to her . . . there'd even been that moment when her hand had pressed his knee, when suddenly they seemed back together. And it went on. It got better. That bloody ring was all ready to go back on her finger. But then he'd tried to kiss her and for some sodding reason she had turned against him again . . .

Why? Why? He had given her promises, asked her forgiveness, almost gone on his knees! And still it was all bloody off-and-on, and she'd shoved the ring back into his hand. He took it from his pocket and scowled at it. So where were they now, just frigging where?

'It's Friday, Mr Kenny. I got you a cod steak . . .'

He jammed the ring back in his pocket. One thing was plain, anyway. She'd be expecting him to carry on with his plans for the house. That way he would be showing he was serious, that he did mean what he said ... that, and the rest! So. He picked up the phone again. But Gwen wasn't back. Where the devil was she?

'Will you be in today, Mr Kenny?'

The black cat was making a habit of the Jag. He chased it off, swearing, and it jumped on a wall and crouched, glaring at him. He slammed into his seat and neglected to belt up – so let some rotten copper book him! – and reversed out of the drive without troubling himself to glance over his shoulder. Fortunately, nothing was passing. He unleashed the Jag with a squeal of tyres. He had half a mind ... no, sod it! Straight up the road. Straight to Gwen's place.

But at once on arriving he knew he'd drawn a blank: an empty drive told the story. To make quite sure he rang the bell, keeping his thumb on the button several moments.

'She told me she was going into town, Mr Wicks!' The face of Gwen's neighbour peered over the fence. 'She was expecting you to ring her, but when you didn't she went in to shop.'

'Did she say when she'd be back?'

'Said to ring her this evening. Said she'd probably call on your mother.'

He got back in the car. Blast, bloody blast! He could chase her into town, but what was the use? If he caught her at all it would be at mum's, and a fat lot of talk they could have together there. He wanted her alone, and not just about the house. About Joyce was why he needed to see her. She understood, could tell him, help him ... she should have been there! Her absence seemed a defection.

Surlily he set the Jag rolling, drove down through the village to the ferry, the sea. Once more he was going nowhere, stuck, isolated, without an aim. He found parking not far from the pub and didn't bother to lock the car. Went in. Ordered a pint. Jammed his arse on a bench among the visitors. Rotten Wicko! He drank, and re-ordered. But it was too early to tie one on.

*

He had his lunch there and felt a bit better, though still with that sense of isolation and bafflement. So close he'd come to climbing out of it yesterday, to getting his foot back on the ladder! Well . . . he wasn't through with it yet. Missing Gwen had been a temporary blip. He would see her again, hear what Dick was recommending, have that heart-to-heart about the puzzle he was in . . . A few hours of delay was all, a bit of patience. And he could spare that.

With better heart, he got back in the Jag and set it rolling, he cared not where. Perhaps a burn-up on the A road . . .? But even that didn't really grab him. In the end he found himself following the route of yesterday, his mind almost a blank, the same roads, the same villages, and finally the wide outlook of the Cliff. Why had she chosen it? As a place where they could talk? But he was sure it went deeper than that. It was where he had brought her when he'd got his first car, and once on a later, a more special occasion . . . She'd remembered it, he knew.

He'd just got a promotion. He'd told her about it on the trip. Then, as they were strolling along the track: 'What do you think, Joycey? Couldn't we?'

'Do you mean what I think you mean?'

'You know I do!'

'Well . . .'

How would she have forgotten it, the place where he proposed? No: it was that which had been in her mind yesterday and to which deliberately she had steered him. So . . . it hadn't quite worked out. But surely the intention must have been there?

He found himself parking again where they'd parked and his steps automatically turning towards the track. Today, Friday, there were fewer visitors, tomorrow being change-over day. He followed the track, step by step, till once more he came to the old yacht. Some kids were climbing over it when he arrived, but they were soon called away by their parents. He sat. Today the tide was higher and his feet were in deeper mud, but he barely noticed. Across the river, the

70

same birds: the same comfortless seat biting into his backside. What had gone wrong? He frowned at the birds. He had tried to kiss her, but wasn't that natural, what any man in his place would have done? Yet she had shrunk from him, gone suddenly tight – why? Had he changed somehow? Did something show . . . ?

He sat a long time scowling at the birds and squelching his feet in the mud, then found himself involuntarily shaking his head – bloody no! No, it couldn't be that. She wasn't ready and he'd tried to rush her, that was what had happened there. He should have held back and given her time. Then it might have been a different story.

And . . . yet.

Bloody no!

He felt water penetrating his shoes. He jumped up swearing, sending helter-skelter a duck that had swum close to him. Sod it, why had he come here? He squelched his way to higher ground, grabbed himself a handful of grass and scrubbed the worst of the mud from his shoes. To hell with it all! Let it work itself out. Either she'd have him or she wouldn't. But the other, that was plain stupid, couldn't have any bearing on the business.

He squelched back to the car, and drove. Pure cussedness made him take the road through the forest. Why not, why not? It was over and he was as free to go that way as anyone else. He hit the trees. He hit the straight. He nearly ran into parked cars. Cars . . . bloody police cars! And bloody policemen, one waving him down! He didn't stop. In his mirror, he saw the man shrug and turn away. Then he was round the next bend and struggling to keep his speed in check.

Had they found it?

It didn't have to be that . . .

For a wild moment, he wasn't in the car at all. Some other person was driving it, a body like his, but that was in another place, barely related.

71

Some sodding exercise . . . the buggers! They'd chosen that spot by pure chance . . .

And the frigger who'd waved him down – he'd been going too fast, all the sod wanted was to tell him off . . .

No, it didn't have to be that. Didn't. Didn't!

It could have been . . .

It could . . .

But he knew it wasn't. All down the road parked cars, bloody people. And back there. By the tank. That was where the buggers were. By the tank – the frigging tank! They were only interested in the tank. They'd found the sod. Found him. A few bloody days, and they'd found him!

And then it was him back there in the car, idling it, driving like some old berk, finding himself leaving the forest, edging his way in the direction of the heath.

Hell, hell, bloody hell!

Was it any use to drive away?

Better to turn round, go back there . . . give himself up and get it over?

He slowed almost to a stop. To get it over, get it off his back! To tell those sods, tell them, shove it off on to them . . . They'd seen it before, knew about these things. They might even understand. Like frigging Lord Muck . . . yes! And then he'd be shot of it. Shot!

But his body drove on. He wasn't going to do it. Bloody mad he'd be to do it! They'd got nothing on him, nothing. No evidence, no witness, no sodding motive. Just a smelly old tramp who someone had strangled and left to pickle in the lousy tank. Leave them to bloody chew on that. It was their job. Let them get on with it. And Wicko, Wicko keep driving away, the lucky one: the winner . . .

Faster now, faster. The heath. The familiar road to the village. The bloody trees disappearing from his mirror, the houses beginning to show ahead. So normal, so stupidly normal, the green, the pond, the ambling ducks, Vera's cottage, the Bell, the little shop. The house.

What was he expecting – a police car parked there?

72

Well there wasn't – no sign of the buggers!

Into the drive then. Into it. Slam the door, and inside . . .

He threw himself down on the hard-arsed sofa, his hands grappling the carved wood. The smell of the place was in his nostrils, the smell of age. A smell that soothed.

So, so . . .

It had to happen some time!

He writhed on the sofa. He'd got to think! The buggers weren't after him, perhaps never would be, only he could give himself away. There'd been no witness, he'd left no clue. No way could they connect what they'd found with him. He was bloody fire-proof. He'd only got to act normal, just be himself, Kenny Wicks, old Wicko.

Frigging simple enough, wasn't it?

Kenny Wicks, the lucky one!

Gwen's brother, Joycey's bloke, mum's boy. Him.

Yes. Simple. Or was it quite as simple as that . . .?

He twisted, grappled, laid his head on his arm, stared at the flowers in the faded carpet. No . . . perhaps it wasn't so simple. It was going to be an act, a bloody act. He'd got to act himself, whoever that was. He'd have to be on his guard every sodding moment – and with mum and Gweny that wouldn't be easy! And Joyce would have her eye on him like an eagle . . . would it still be possible to carry on with Joyce? Maybe, maybe not. And Vera, she was a sharp one too. And that lot at the Bell, including . . . And Sandra, lousy Sandra!

He went very still. What was it he'd said to her? He must have been crazy – off his nut! She hadn't believed him, of course, made out he was just another stupid punter, but that was then. Now, when the news from the forest hit the fan . . . He almost wrenched the carving from the sofa. How could he have been so bloody dumb? Too much to hope she would have forgotten it! And if the police came round, questioning . . .

Well, he'd just have to pass it off, the sort of silly thing you said to tarts. It didn't prove a sodding thing and they could make what they liked of it, couldn't they?

73

And the odds were, that being a tart . . .

No. Forget it. Forget it!

'Oh . . . you're back then, Mr Kenny!'

He almost started from the sofa. Vera stood there, concern, surprise in her face as she looked at him.

'You're all right, are you, Mr Kenny?'

'Yes . . . yes. I'm all right, Vera.'

'Only you seemed . . .'

'Never mind that! I was just having a bit of a rest.'

'Well . . .'

He cursed himself. This, at the very first encounter! Still with a puzzled expression on her face she stooped to pick up the antimacassar that had fallen down.

'Am I to cook the cod then?'

'The cod . . . yes, please!'

'It'll keep till tomorrow if you'd rather, Mr Kenny.'

'No, Vera. I'll have it tonight.'

'I'll get it on, then.'

She went. He sat clenching and unclenching his hands. For Christ's sake he must pull himself together, put on a face, act sodding normal! It was going to work out. There was nothing to be afraid of, nothing that would ever come back to him. All he had to do was sit it out, be one of the audience, keep his cool . . .

He went through to the kitchen.

'Like a sherry, Vera?'

'Well, I wouldn't say no, Mr Kenny!'

'I think we deserve one.'

'That's very kind of you . . .'

'Go on! What would I do without you?'

He poured them brimming glasses and touched her glass with his own before drinking. He caught her eye – now it had a twinkle in it! – and managed to respond with a smile.

'How about another one?'

'I shouldn't really . . .'

'Like I said, we deserve it!'

The cod, when it came, was prime, and he succeeded in eating every last scrap of it.

'They say it was kids who found him. It was on the six o'clock news. They saw something floating in the tank out there and got their people to have a look. Didn't you hear the news?'

'I've been out all day . . .'

'Around lunch-time this happened. I expect they were having a picnic there – I'll bet they won't do that again in a hurry!'

'Did they . . . say who he was?'

'Some elderly bloke. That's all they're saying at the moment.'

He drank, and stared at his glass. He hadn't wanted to show up at the Bell. After Vera left his whole instinct had been to stay where he was, stay under cover. But it wouldn't do, wasn't natural. The buggers had seen him, back at the forest. They'd seen him and knew that he'd seen them, and if he hadn't turned up here to share in the gossip . . . In the end, bold as brass, he'd pushed his way into the bar, swaggered across to the counter and ordered his usual pint from Sid. His fear that Lord Muck might be there was unfounded. It was just the regulars, and not so many of them. And they seemed quieter, talking together in low voices as they huddled round the tables. At the counter was just himself and Biker Jack, the latter with his stubbly face frowning.

'I suppose he couldn't have fallen in . . .?'

'Doesn't sound like it, Jack. Not the way they talk about it.'

'He could have done it on purpose.'

'Could've, I suppose. But you get the impression there was more to it.'

'Some bugger did for him.'

'Sounds like it.'

'You don't get much of that. Not round here.'

'There's always a first time. What do you think, Wicko?'

Wicks shrugged. 'Like you say.'

75

'Perhaps he was just dumped there,' Sid said. 'Some sod who knew about the tank. He could have been knocked off anywhere. The tank would seem like a good place to hide him. Just that bastard's bit of bad luck that the kids were horsing about there.'

'I wonder.' Biker frowned. 'Do they know when it happened?'

'Didn't say,' Sid said. 'I dare say they'll have an idea.'

Biker drank. 'I'm thinking,' he said. 'Last week there was a traveller camped out that way. Just up the road, you know. Where they used to park before the hurricane.'

Sid stared. 'You think there's a connection?'

'He looked a right bastard,' Biker said. 'On his own he was, in one of those old vans. I saw him there a couple of times.'

'Is he still there?'

Biker shook his head. 'Wouldn't expect him to be, would you?'

'Well, I don't know,' Sid said. 'I suppose it's an idea.'

'Some frigger had to do it, didn't they.'

'It's a question of when it was done,' Sid said, 'I reckon. Until we know that we're just guessing.'

Biker frowned at Wicks. 'Did you see him?' he said. 'Weren't you round that way Monday?'

'. . . Monday?'

'Around lunch-time. Didn't I see you heading that way?'

Somehow . . . somehow . . .! Wicks tilted his glass. 'Monday . . . yes. Yes, I was round there.'

'And you didn't see him?'

'No . . .'

'He was there when I passed,' Biker said. 'Tucked in a bit, you may have missed him. But it's a sure thing the bugger has gone now.'

'Fill you up?' Sid said. 'You're empty.'

Silently, Wicks pushed his glass across the counter.

Sid filled him, went to serve another customer. Biker took time off to light a fag. Hell, hell, bloody hell! Wicks stared and stared at his glass. He'd been seen, and he couldn't deny it –

76

now he was nailed there, nailed to the spot! While frigging worse, up the road ... Could the fellow have seen ... Could he?

'You hear that? They're going to use the Parish Hall as their incident-room. Frany just told me – he's the clerk. Should be a few extra customers, eh?'

But he wasn't listening, couldn't listen, could barely get the glass to his lips. If – if – ! If ... But surely the bloody bloke would have said something, done something! And up there, up the road, it was too far away ... no, he couldn't have been a witness! Just hang on, stick to the tale ... so he'd taken in the forest on his way home ... thought of getting lunch at Grimchurch ... changed his mind. Yes, that was the tale!

'Oho ... now we'll hear what's what!'

What the hell was bloody Sid on about now?

The door had just opened. Wicks started round.

Bloody Lord Muck had walked into the bar.

'Pour me a dram, Sid.'

He wasn't smiling tonight. Instead, he had a rather solemn look on his square-featured face. He took a measured sip from the glass Sid handed him, then turned and set his back against the counter. And he had his audience, oh yes! Every face in the bar was turned towards him.

'I suppose you people know what happened here today?'

No question about that: you might have heard a pin drop.

'In case you haven't, the body of a man was discovered in Grimchurch Forest. It had been placed in a static water-tank at a corner of the picnic area. Well, the local police have pursued their enquiries and we know now when the incident occurred. That being so, we are in a position to invite witnesses to come forward. The man, I should tell you, was a mendicant, his age about sixty-five, grey hair, grey beard, five feet six inches in height, and wearing a stained black coat, ragged jeans and trainer shoes. On his back he carried a shabby pack. He was last seen in Grimchurch at noon on

77

Monday, where a lady gave him a pack of sandwiches. We have since obtained medical evidence that he consumed these shortly before his death. So, if anyone here saw this man at any time after noon on Monday, they may be in possession of significant testimony and we are asking them to come forward!

A hand shot up . . . some louse!

'Yes?'

'May we ask if this man was murdered?'

The sod paused . . . bloody paused! 'Yes. I think I may answer that question. The medical evidence confirms that he died from violent strangulation. There was no evidence of a struggle. He would appear to have been taken by surprise.'

Silence! Then: 'But . . . why did they do it?'

'As yet we have no knowledge of the motive. It could well have been a psychopathic killing, which makes it all the more urgent for us to arrest the culprit. Such people have been known to repeat their crimes. So, if you can help us, we urge you to do so.'

Now a murmuring, the sods looking at each other, fiddling with their glases . . . but no takers! Because why . . .? He could have told them!

'Were any of you in the forest that day?'

Sid's eyes were switching between him and Biker. He shook his head at Sid, but that stupid Biker, his eyes staring . . .

'On Monday of this week?'

'Yes – I was!'

Out, out it came. He couldn't help it, the great berk, his blubber-lips wouldn't hold it in.

'You are?'

'. . . Jack Stringer.'

'Oh yes! The gentleman with the Speed-Twin. And you were in the forest on Monday?'

'Yes . . . Monday. About when you say.'

'At about noon?'

'A bit later it was. Could've been getting towards one.'

'And you took that route – past the picnic area?'

'Yes. I was going that way.'

Greasy tangle of hair, ancient leather jacket: the mild, teasing eyes were taking him in: T-shirt, chinos, boots, the puffed, pallid features nestled in stubble. Fifty or more the sod had to be. He lived alone in a cottage his parents had left him. Him and his bike, a sodding relic, a left-over from the days of rock'n' roll . . .

'Perhaps you'll tell us about it, Mr Stringer.'

'Well, I was going that way . . .'

'And you noticed something?'

He nodded.

'What?'

'Well . . . him. The bloke they found out there.'

'You saw the victim?'

'Yuh. Saw him. Sitting on a bench there, eating his nosh.'

Bloody, bloody hell!

'This would be the picnic area?'

'Yuh. I cast my eye in there, going past. I wasn't in a hurry. Nearly stopped to have a word with the old bugger, but then I carried on.'

'And – he was alone?' Mucker's eyes were tight on the frigger.

'I didn't see nobody else.'

'And you passed nobody?'

'Not there, I didn't. There was some cars parked further on.'

'But . . . in that area?'

'Going to tell you, aren't I?' Bloody Biker gave himself a hitch on his stool. 'That sodding traveller. He was still there. He's gone now, but he was there on Monday.'

Empty! How came his glass was empty?

'What traveller was that?'

'Why, one of those. Rough he looked. Got a big old van. It was stuck there at the old spot, behind the trees. But you could see it if you looked.'

'You mean, the old picnic area.'

'Yuh. It's only just along the road. He'd been there a week, I do know. But he wasn't there on Tuesday.'

Mucker's eyes turned to the others in the bar. 'Did anyone else here notice that van?'

'Yes – I did!' One of the posh wrinklies: he got to his feet, approached the counter.

'And you are . . .?'

'Arthur Trafford. I live at The Elms in Miller's Loke. I saw that van there last week and meant to have a word with the Forestry about it.'

'Would you have seen it there on Monday?'

The wrinkly shook his head. 'This was Friday. I was going that way to town. I stopped to take a good look. An old Austin Princess ambulance conversion, wings, headlamps, the lot, and painted green and cream. Quite a vintage vehicle, it was.'

'Did you speak to its owner?'

'Rather not! I have to say his attitude was less than encouraging. He was a man of about forty, hefty build, lank fair hair, an aggressive manner. I don't think he'd washed lately. I felt that perhaps we had little in common.'

'And – the van's registration?'

'Sorry. But it was one that preceded date-letters.'

Mucker sipped his dram and looked around. 'Anyone else with information?'

He could feel bloody Sid's stare on him . . . bloody Sid! And then frigging Biker . . .

'Me . . . I was round that way on Monday . . .'

'You, Mr Wicks?'

He nodded. 'I was driving back – from London – and thought I'd go to the Anchor for lunch . . .'

Out, it was out! And those sodding eyes . . . was it possible Mucker had checked up on him?

'What time would that have been, Mr Wicks?'

'I don't know . . . getting on for one. I think I passed Biker up the road somewhere, he'll tell you if you ask.'

'Up at the junction,' Biker said. 'He couldn't have gone through much after me.'

'A few minutes later?'

'Couldn't have been more. It's only a mile, if it's that.'

80

'So . . .?' The eyes were back.

'I – I didn't see anything, did I?'

'Not at the picnic area?'

'No. All I'd got on my mind was lunch.'

Mucker paused. 'Let's get it straight,' he said. 'Are you saying that you didn't see the victim, or that you wouldn't have noticed him?'

'I . . . wouldn't have noticed him. I didn't look, just had my eyes on the road.'

'You saw no one.'

'No. No one.'

'You didn't notice the van.'

He shook his head.

'Well . . . in that case!' Mucker gave a slight shrug. 'Thank you for your information, Mr Wicks. Perhaps tomorrow you'll call in at the Parish Rooms and give a statement to the officer there.' He turned back to Biker and the wrinkly. 'I must ask you two gentlemen to come with me now. You have information which may be significant and we need statements from you without delay.'

'Only too pleased,' the wrinkly said. 'The sooner you nab this villain the better.'

'It was that sodding traveller,' Biker said. 'I'll bet a pint on it with anyone.'

They accompanied Mucker out. It was done. He'd put it across him. But bloody Christ, he needed a drink – something with a bit more sting than bitter!

'A double Scotch, Sid . . .'

He drank, drank, about him the surf of excited conversation.

'Another . . .'

Then why – why was it? This feeling that he was still on the edge of a precipice?

He was in the clear! Let them do their stuff, take bloody statements till they dropped. Wicko, old Wicko was in the clear, they weren't going to have him, today, never! Only . . . sod it! . . . he'd better stay sober. Better had . . .

And he was feeling for his wallet.

81

6

'You are Mr Kenneth Wicks of the Old Manse, Welbourne . . .?'

It had taken aspirin to get him off the night before. He had been half-cut, but that wasn't enough, couldn't stop his mind turning over and over.

One thought had been dogging him – that of the traveller, whose van had been parked only a stone's-throw away. If he'd been on the stroll for some stupid reason he might have seen something . . . seen enough! Because it didn't need much. Just the Jag pulling in there, or leaving again. That would do, give Lord Muck all he needed to drop his mit on Wicko's shoulder. He could swear the sod was lying, of course, just trying to shift the blame . . . but no, he knew that would never stick! Not with those eyes of Mucker's watching him . . .

'At approximately twelve thirty p.m. on Monday . . .'

Finally he had succumbed and taken the aspirin, and even then it had seemed for ever until his mind ran down, began to lose the thread. But in the end it did work and he slept. Slept solid till Vera woke him. Stood there smiling with his cup of tea – 'I thought you never were going to wake up, Mr Kenny!' And perhaps it would have been as well if he hadn't . . .

'What's the time, Vera?'

'After nine, Mr Kenny. I've just been listening to the news.'

'The news . . .?'

'It was all on there – you know, that body they found yesterday. Well, they're looking for a gypsy fellow in a van. It seems he was about there when it happened. Do you think he could have done it?'

'Have . . . they found him?'

'No, not yet. They're asking people for information. And they've got a description of the van – a big old green-and-yellow job. I suppose you never saw it when you were about there?'

He shook his head and drank tea.

'It was the day you came back from London when it happened, so the police say.'

'What about it, Vera?'

'Just saying, Mr Kenny. Sometimes you drive round through the forest.'

'Well . . . I didn't see it!'

'No, there you are then! What would you like for breakfast, Mr Kenny?'

Sullenly he drank his tea. Did even Vera suspect him? And the bloody traveller . . . it couldn't be long before they got their hands on him. He would have to expect it. They were going to come back to him. And then he would have to face it out . . . sod it, sod it! All he could hope for was that the bloke had stayed tucked in his van . . .

'You saw no one in the neighbourhood of the picnic area . . .'

When the phone went, he could feel his heart jump. But it was only mum. He'd forgotten to ring her . . . Mum, who wanted to hear about Joyce!

'You might have let me know how it went, Kenny. Instead I had to hear it from her mother. She seems to think it might be on again – at least, that was the impression she got from Joyce.'

Was it? And did it matter? Suddenly, Joyce had dropped out of the reckoning, belonged to another world. What was the use of talking about Joyce?

'Are you coming over?'

'Mum . . .'

'I want to hear it from you, Kenny.'

'Oh . . . all right!'

'I'll expect you to lunch, then. I've ordered a chicken for the weekend.'

Another sodding world. If only they realized! Mum, Gweny

83

and the rest. His daft money, too . . . where had it got him? What was it worth?'

'If you will just read it through, sir, and sign it here . . .'

He hesitated, there, in that bleak Parish Room. What was he signing? His eyes wouldn't take it in, the words were dancing on the paper. His damnation, like as not! But it was too late to change his tale now. And even if he did . . . He grabbed the pen and scribbled his name where the man had indicated.

'That will be all, sir. And thank you for assisting us.'

He got up and left the building in a daze. Something final about it, that statement . . . wasn't it more like a confession he was leaving there?

He needed a drink, but the pub wasn't open. Instead, he strolled by the pond and the quacking ducks. For how much longer . . . He stood staring, feeling the sun hot on his head. Alone. He was bloody alone. Not a soul now he could turn to. And it was the same if the sods came for him or if they never got a smell. That, that was what he'd done back there, he'd put himself here: on the outside. A ghost, a nothing. A nobody. Less than the thing he'd stuffed in the tank . . .

Pull your bloody self together, Wicko!

He kicked at a duck that had waddled too close, turned about, strode across the green, past the Jag, into the house.

'I'll be out, Vera. I'm lunching at mum's.'

'That's all right, Mr Kenny. I was only going to make you an omelette.'

The cat had seen him coming. It fled into the bushes and crouched there, its eyes large.

Saturday traffic held him up and he was swearing as he entered the town, and when he turned down Pier Avenue he found most of the parking already taken. There was space by the Clements house, but he ignored it – he was in no mood for an encounter with Joyce! Today was her Saturday 'on', he knew, but the odds were that she would be back for lunch. So he drove by and cruised along the Front till a departing car offered him a space. That was away up by the lighthouse, but so what? He nearly didn't lock the car . . .

'You're late, Kenny. And if I didn't know you better, I might think you were trying to avoid me.'

The same hall, the same rooms, the same smell coming from the kitchen . . . shouldn't something have changed, somewhere? At least she could have put away dad's hat!

'So now tell me. Is it on again?'

'We did spend the day together, mum.'

'Then why are you being so secret about it, Kenny? You could at least have rung me and let me know.'

'Well . . . things.'

'Look me in the eye, son.'

'We . . . talked about it. You know! About the house, that sort of thing. There was a lot we had to talk over.'

'And what exactly does that mean?'

'Well . . . everything!'

'And everything is nothing, my son. Is she having you back?'

'Yes . . . I mean . . .'

His mother jerked her head impatiently. 'I can tell you what it means. It means she isn't sure you're being serious yet. And you can't blame her, Kenny. You've a lot to answer for.'

'Oh, mum . . . !'

'It's true, isn't it? The way you've behaved would sicken any woman. And Joyce is a long way from being that. She's the sort of girl you can put your trust in.'

'I know, I know!'

'So what are you going to do about it?'

'Mum, I've promised her – '

'That isn't enough.'

'Then what can I do?'

Her eyes fastened on his. 'I'll tell you, Kenny. You can come home.'

'Come . . . home?'

'You heard me.'

'But – !'

'Your room here is all ready. You've only to fetch your

85

things. You can move back in today.'

He could only gaze at her. 'But why!'

'Why? I should think that's plain enough, isn't it? You've got to show her you mean what you say, that you're really going to turn over a new leaf. So come back home, son. Let her see you're serious. It's the only way you're going to do it. If you stop where you are she's always going to have doubts, but if you're back here she'll feel easier in her mind. Can't you see that?'

'Mum . . . I don't know!'

'I think you do, Kenny. I think you do.'

'But the house . . . I can't just leave it!'

'Oh yes you can. It won't run away.'

Why – why was she doing this? For a moment his whole being was in a state of flux. He wanted it – yes, he wanted it! – to sink back like that, into home . . . everything. To be back with himself, with . . . Wasn't it the answer, to come back here? To leave that . . . thing . . . over there at the house, a memory, a bad dream . . . nothing? Yes, if it would stay there. If it would!

'Perhaps . . . you're right, mum.'

'I know I'm right. If you still want Joyce, there's no other way. And tomorrow she's off. We'll ask her round here. Then you'll see what a difference it will make.'

'But . . . today?'

'Why not today?'

'Well . . . things. Things I've got to take care of!'

She clicked her tongue. 'There can't be so many! And you can take care of them when you fetch your clothes.'

'Well, yes. I suppose . . .'

She nodded determinedly. 'First, we'll have lunch. Then you can help me make up the bed. I'll put a bottle in it, just in case, but I think the mattress is well aired.'

'Mum . . .'

'Come on, now. There's the table to set before I dish up.'

Was it possible? Already, it seemed, he was slotting back into that familiar household – no longer a guest, a visitor, but himself, Kenny Wicks, the son of the house. Setting the table he was an insider, the plates, the cutlery belonging with him ... could he really believe it? Even the rotten Jag was stuck away, up in the town ...

'Shall we have the news on?'

He froze. 'Do you want it?'

'There may be something fresh about that man they found. You heard about it, did you? But of course, you must have done! They'll be talking of nothing else in the village.'

'Well ...'

Providentially it was brief, shots of the forest, the tank, the police: a plain-clothes copper he didn't know requesting news of any sightings of the van.

But then: 'Look – isn't that your Scotland Yard man – the one who's got a house in the village? Gwen was telling me about him – now I remember! His name is Chief Superintendent Gently. I suppose you haven't met him?'

Bugger. Bugger! 'He was in the pub last night.'

'Did he speak to you, Kenny?'

'Well ... yes. He was asking questions, wanted to know something.'

'Oh Kenny! And you could tell him?'

'Mum, it wasn't anything, really! Seems I was driving past there on Monday, when they think it happened. So I might have seen something.'

'And did you?'

'No, I didn't! I didn't meet or see anyone. I had to sign a statement for them this morning, for any good it's going to do.'

'But you were there – in the forest!'

'I tell you, I didn't see a thing.'

'But you might have done.'

'Only I didn't.'

'It could have been going on right when you were there.'

'Oh ... Mum!'

She shook her head. 'Aren't you just a little bit excited about it, Kenny? I would be. To think I was there when it might

87

have been happening a few yards away. Didn't you even see the van they talk about?'

'No, I didn't see that either!'

'And that poor tramp?'

'Mum, please!'

'Well, I don't know. You seem to take it very calmly.'

He sank his face over his plate. Tell her? Should he bloody tell her? He could feel her eyes probing him, curious, questioning. He'd play it wrong. He should have come out with it before they saw it on the news – yes! He could see that now. It should have been the first thing he told her.

'Do you think it was the gypsy fellow who did it?'

'I don't know! It's him they're after.'

'But what made him do such a thing? I mean, the man was only a poor old tramp.'

'He – may have had reasons.'

'But what reasons? Would you want to kill a tramp, Kenny?'

'I'm not him. The bloke may have upset him – perhaps the gypo caught him nicking something from his van.'

'And for that he would strangle him?'

'May have done.'

She was shaking her head again. 'I can't believe that. He would have to have been a – what is it they call them? A psycho-something.'

'Perhaps . . . he was.'

She gave a little shudder. 'Then the sooner they put him inside the better! It makes you feel creepy. He could do it again. And the next time it could be – well, anyone.'

'Mum . . . please let it drop!'

'It's all right for you, Kenny. But a woman like me, living on her own – '

'Mum, I've had enough of it! I had to go through all that this morning.'

'Then you should understand.'

'I do! But just now I've got other things on my mind.'

She gave him a sharp look, then went on with her lunch. What was the use of trying to deceive her? it was as though she could smell a lie ten yards off, could spot it before he ever opened his mouth. And now she knew where he'd been at the critical moment and must be guessing he hadn't been quite straight with her about it . . . If he came back here, how long would it take her? How long before she dragged it out of him? No: he daren't. Daren't give her the opportunity. If he came back here there could be only one end to it . . .

'Mum . . .'

'Yes?'

'Perhaps not quite tonight, mum. There's so much to see to – about the house.'

'Can't you see to it from here?'

'No . . . not really! I've got to talk to those people, show them what I want done. Gwen's been arranging it, I can't let her down. Perhaps . . . later on! When it's all been settled.'

'Look at me, Kenny.'

'Oh, mum!'

'You don't want to come home, do you?'

'Yes, I do., But – '

She shook her head. 'I've been waiting to hear what excuse you'd come up with.' She paused, her grey eyes measuring him. 'There's something wrong, son, isn't there? I noticed it when you walked in here. You haven't been acting like yourself at all. Are you in trouble, Kenny?'

'No, mum!'

'You don't have to lie to me, you know.'

'Oh, mum . . .!'

'You can talk to me. That's what mothers are all about.'

'Mum – please!'

She gazed a long time. 'Well, when you're ready, son. When you're ready. I'm here, you know that. Just don't treat me like a fool.'

'There's nothing, mum. Really!'

'Hand me your plate. I've made an apple tart for pudding.'

Dare he walk out? But no, he couldn't: he had to sit on through that meal. And she let it drop, talked about Gwen, about Flo expecting a baby. Then Joyce again . . . when was he going to see her, remembering that tomorrow was Sunday? Should she ask her to tea? If he would take her advice, he would strike again while the iron was hot . . .

At last, at long last . . .

'And just remember, son. I'm always here.'

Then the door closed behind him and he was back on the street.

Alone.

He found his way into a pub, ordered and downed a quick half. Yes . . . bloody alone! It wasn't to be. Never, never could he run back there for cover. It had beckoned, had almost claimed him, but then that frigging thing had reached out . . . Was it always going to be like that, the thing crushing him, driving him back to his nowhere? He spat and ordered another half. And she had thought . . . just like Lord Muck! The deed of a psycho, a bloody psycho . . . but he wasn't one – no, he wasn't! It hadn't needed a psycho. Just a poor lousy sod. A sod who'd been treated like filth. Driven to it. Him. Who, before that, had never as much as kicked a dog. He flung back more beer. It wasn't fair! Wasn't there, somewhere, a bugger who would understand? He wasn't a criminal, it had somehow happened, him being in the wrong place at the wrong time . . .

'Can I do you a top-up?'

'Sod off!'

He nearly threw the glass at the stupid bloke. And the bloke looked ugly for a moment, looked as though he was going to ask for it. His fingers itched. Could he be a psycho . . .? But he slammed the glass down and walked out. Sod them, bloody sod them! If they made him feel that way, who was to blame?

He walked across the Front and leaned on the rail, stared down at the beach, the placid sea. Kids were bathing, trippers sitting on the sand, a woman walking with her dog. The seaside in rotten August . . . and him leaning there, with his millions behind him! Wasn't there a way he could buy himself

90

out, throw the stuff about till they got off his back? Twenty years, that was a life sentence, and you could cut it down to half. Lay a million on the line . . . that travelling geezer might jump at it. And the police, were they virgin white? They were bloody human like the rest of us! Up the ante . . . two million. Three. The dosh was there – they were dealing with Wicko! He spat over the rail. But wasn't that just the snag? They were dealing with Wicko . . . poor, sodding Wicko . . .

'Could you tell me, please . . .?'

glared at the woman, whose eyes were suddenly frightened.

'I just wanted to ask you the way to the toilets!'

He jerked a finger: she hastened away.

No . . . it wasn't going to work! He turned his back on the murmur of the sea. Nothing was going to work, not if that traveller spewed his guts up. Then it was one word against another, with the tart maybe putting in her spoke too. They were going to have him, twenty stinking years – you could forget the good behaviour! The traveller had only to have seen him pulling in there: it didn't need any more than that.

He stood long, his back to the railings, scowling at the flower-beds that lined the front.

But perhaps – wasn't it just possible? – the traveller had been in his van all the time? He had told the truth when he said he'd seen no one. He hadn't met or caught a glimpse of a soul . . . no! The scene sprang to his mind, the vacant area, the empty road. That's how it had been all the time he was there, when he'd driven in, when he'd driven away – he could swear to it: there had been no witness. And with the van down the road, hidden behind trees . . . No, he wasn't quite done yet: just had to carry on, keep putting a good face on it!

At last he heaved himself off the rails and headed for the lighthouse and the Jag. Once again he found a note tucked under his wiper, and once again he tore it up and jettisoned the pieces.

'I'm not hungry, Vera. Don't bother to cook for me.'

91

There hadn't been a copper waiting outside the house. The village, the green looked as peaceful as ever, and the cat had risen lazily from the wall when he parked.

'There's only cheese, Mr Kenny.'

'That'll do.'

'I can do you a bit of salad.'

'I'll have some fruit.'

'Well, if you say so . . .'

'Oh, and it's Saturday, Vera. I was almost forgetting!'

He paid her wages, adding a ten, and after brewing up for him she departed. There was something of mum about Vera, trotting away to her cottage across the green, the same sturdy, independent little figure, with her bag hugged under her arm. He watched her till she reached her door, saw her fumble for her key and let herself in. Had she guessed something too? She was concerned about him, he knew. With her, with everyone, he had to watch his step, act normal, give nothing away . . .

He ate in the kitchen. It was news time again, but he couldn't bring himself to face the television. Rather, he would sit here, in Vera's domain, gazing out of the window at the tangle of garden. So things were happening – could he stop them? Perhaps it was better if he didn't know. Better if he didn't even think about it, just forced his mind to stay empty until . . . He thought of Gwen, who'd be expecting him to ring her, but he couldn't face that either. Her husband would be there, Dick, wanting him to talk about . . . no!

He watched the garden, watched the birds, watched the cat creeping through the grass, drank tea from a pot that had gone cold, found the setting sun beginning to dazzle his eyes. And in the pub . . . would that dangerous sod be there, primed with fresh matter, fresh questions? Perhaps wondering why Wicko was sitting at home alone and not propping up the bar, his ears flapping for news . . .? Yes, he bloody might be! So? So . . .?

He shoved his crockery in the sink. No option! He'd have to

face him, stare the bastard straight in the eyes . . .

His nerve held. He tramped down the green, past the ducks, up to the door. He flung it open a little too hard, so that it banged against its stop. And went in.

'Wicko . . . take it easy! You don't have to knock the blinking place down.'

'Sorry, Sid . . .'

'I should think so!'

And the sod, the rotten sod, wasn't there.

'Have you got some news then, Wicko?'

'News . . .?'

'Ah. The way you came through the door, I thought you might have heard something fresh, like what's happening about that gypo bloke.

'Him – what about him?'

'Hadn't you heard? They came across him camped out in Latchford Chase. The Super was in here earlier. Said they got word from the Forestry out there.'

'And . . . he's been arrested?'

'What do you think! They'll be bringing him back here, we reckon. The Super was chuffed. If you ask me, he thinks they've got this business tied up. But you haven't heard anything?'

'No . . . I've been out.'

'A pity you weren't in here a bit sooner.'

Mechanically, Sid was drawing a pint. Just as mechanically, Wicks accepted it and drank. The bar was buzzing, but he scarcely noticed it, nor the stubbly face of Biker at his elbow.

'So what do you reckon, then. Did he do it?'

'Of course he bloody did!' Biker put in. 'I saw him, don't forget. He was just the rotten sod to do a job like that.'

'But what got into him?'

'Ask me another. With crap like that, do you need a reason? He may have just seen the old bloke sitting there and thought he made the place look untidy.'

'Go on, Jack! What do you say, Wicko?'

Wicks shook his head and drank.

'Must have been later,' Biker said. 'After you went through there, Wicko. He sat eating his nosh when I passed and you couldn't have been more than five minutes after me. And you never saw nothing?'

'I . . . wasn't looking that way.'

'You must have noticed something, if that was going on!'

'Well I didn't.'

'So it was after,' Biker said. 'When you'd gone. When the place was quiet. The sod may have been poaching or something up that way, and then came out on the old bloke.'

'Could be,' Sid said. 'You may have something, Jack.'

'Wouldn't put nothing past him,' Biker said. 'The old bloke catches him with a brace of pheasants and the gun, so he puts him away. It's happened before.'

'Yeah,' Sid said. 'That could be it. You should have a word with the Super, Jack.'

'I may do. And I may not. Don't forget I was there – it could put me in the running!'

'You soft sod!' Sid said. 'And that would go for you too, Wicko. Or haven't you knocked off any tramps lately?'

'That . . . isn't bloody funny!'

'Keep your wool on, mate – just a joke! Let's be having your glass.'

Had he emptied it already? He shoved the glass across the counter. No, he didn't like the way that Biker was looking at him . . . They'd both been there, that's what the eyes said, and if he, Biker hadn't done it, then . . . He grabbed the filled glass.

'Anyway . . . they've got him.'

'Latchford Chase,' Sid said. 'He hadn't got far. Dare say he didn't think the body would turn up. It could have been safe where he put it for years.'

'Yes . . .'

'His bit of bad luck. What about you, Jack? Ready for another?'

Wicks drank, drank, and drank up. 'Think I'll have an early

night, Sid,' he said. He wrestled with the wad in his pocket, got out a fifty and threw it on the counter. Sid looked at it. He looked at Wicks. He beckoned him to the corner of the counter.

'Listen, Wicko! I was going to tell you this. Watch how you're throwing those things around. The Super was asking me this evening if I'd changed fifties for anyone lately.'

'He asked . . .?'

Sid nodded. 'They found one. In the tank. Along with the bloke. Of course I didn't mention your name – I don't want to make trouble! But I thought I should warn you. Okay?'

'Yes . . . okay, Sid.'

'Perhaps you've got a fiver instead of this?'

Somehow he found a fiver among the rest and crammed the fifty back in his pocket. Sid gave him a wink. He took his change. Then he was outside the pub.

He burned them right there, in the grate in the sitting-room – the chimney must have needed sweeping, because smoke billowed out and made his eyes water. How much was it? He didn't count. Two thousand, three, four – what the hell did it matter? Red, smouldering flames licked round them, scorched them, devoured them. Every bloody fifty-pound note he possessed, he stirred them, watched them crumble, swearing at the smoke that filled the room, stirring, watching till the last one was ashes.

Anything else? Yes – a note for Vera! His shaking hand would scarcely inscribe it. But there it was . . . a few days where? Torquay, rotten Torquay! They could look for him there till hell froze over . . .

Then his bag. Then . . .

The boot of the Jag was locked. Swearing, he flung the bag on the back seat, jumped in, inserted the key and set the engine rolling. Under that bonnet one hundred and forty . . . let it go, let it go! Tyres squealed, the Jag leaped forward and the houses of the village took flight behind him. Wicko was away . . .

And, ahead of him, one road led into another.

7

'If you will just take your place at a table, sir, I'll bring it to you when it's ready. I'm afraid the papers haven't arrived yet, but they should be here any minute.'

Flatness, incredible flatness: fields following fields to a rulered skyline. It had been dark when he pulled in there and he hadn't seen what sort of place he'd come to. Simply, the lights of the Little Chef had beckoned and he'd felt tired, so bloody tired. Where it was he didn't know, didn't care, he'd simply pulled in and asked for a room. Then he'd flaked out on the bed without even taking off his shoes.

'Here's your tea, sir. The other won't be long.'

And, unbelievably, he'd slept . . . gone out like a sodding light! To wake up here, in a place so foreign that he could only sit staring at it through the steamy windows. Flat . . . how could anywhere be so flat? The sea at home was never as flat as this. The sea-horizon loomed high, held a curve in it, while this . . . He shook his head and poured some tea.

'Here you are then, sir! Shall I fetch the mustard?'

'What do they call this place, miss?'

'What – ? Oh, I see! These are the Fens out here, sir. Haven't you been here before?'

And memory stirred. Yes . . .! But so long ago, such an age of time. In his nostrils suddenly a smell . . . the smell of dad's old Super Minx! Packed in the back there, him and the girls, on a journey that seemed to go on for ever . . . three had he been? Not much older! And they'd stopped somewhere here for the loo. He stared and stared. Now he remembered! They had been on that famous holiday to the hills – to the Lakes, that's where they'd been heading . . . Dad had won something, perhaps on the Pools . . .

'Here's the mustard, sir.'

How could he have forgotten – thrust a memory like that into hazy oblivion? It had been their single excursion from the familiar places, their one adventure into foreign parts. He had never been so far away since then. Once, he'd taken mum on a fortnight to Brighton. For the rest, he'd been content . . . only Flo and her husband took their holidays abroad!

And now, by sheer bloody chance – because last night he hadn't given a thought to where he was going – by sheer bloody chance he had taken this road that dad had driven before him.

Or . . . was it chance?

He began to eat, frowning at the food on his plate. Here could have been the spot, the very spot, where they had climbed out and made that rush for the loo . . .

'The papers are here, sir. Would you like me to fetch you one?'

Hell, oh bloody hell! So he wasn't on holiday, and he had best remember it . . . he got up and went to fetch the papers himself.

But it was Sunday, dead-and-alive Sunday, when the local papers didn't publish. After breakfast he ploughed through reams of the others and came up only with a single paragraph. He wasn't important enough, him! His piffling crime wasn't worth a headline. Though perhaps if they'd known . . . for a moment he felt an urge to get on the phone to the sods. He went over the paragraph several times, but only the traveller got a mention. His stupid name was Obadiah Hearne and he was reported to be assisting the police. Assisting the bastards . . . but how much? And with Mucker's penetrating eyes fixed on him. Already the police may have been round to his house, questioning Vera, reading that note . . .

He stuffed the papers in a bin. Just now, at all events, he was safe! Torquay was where they would be hunting for him, not a Little Chef stuck out in the Fens. And after all, that sodding fifty they'd found ... if they could have traced it, they would have done so long since. So they hadn't. It might point to him, but it went no further than that. No: he was safe for the moment. And if he stayed clear of them ... who knew?

'Will you be wanting the room tonight, sir?'

He paid up with harmless tens, then drifted the Jag to the pumps and filled her tank to the very brim. Going where? He still didn't know. Just that it wasn't bloody Torquay. He couldn't even be bothered to look at a map to see where this lousy road was leading him.

'If you're going north, sir ...'

He glared at the man.

'There's still that jam on the A1(M). You can avoid it by going through Doncaster.'

'Thanks so bloody much.'

'Just thought I'd tell you, sir!'

But it struck a note. 'Is the A1 far?'

'Straight down the road, sir, till you come to Newark. Can't be more than sixty from here.'

Should he have given even so much away? Ten to one the man would remember him again! But the A1 ran south as well as north, and they would be lucky to pick him up from a tip so vague ...

He felt the man's eyes were on the Jag as he idled it to the road and signalled his turn. When it came, he drove away unsensationally and only put his foot down when the place had vanished from his mirror. Then he let it rip. He reached Newark within the hour and peeled off down the slip-road to the A1(M). There the road was dualled, and he could really spin ... bloody Scotland, here Wicko comes!

But the A1 was nearly his undoing, and that sodding jam was at the bottom of it. He had taken a chance and ignored the turn-off to Doncaster and then, ten minutes later, was in the thick of it.

'I'll see your licence, sir, if I may.'

For nearly an hour he'd been sitting there, grid-locked. Out of six bloody carriageways there was only one in use, divided between traffic going north and traffic going south. Did they have to do this, on a frigging August Sunday, with holiday traffic at a peak? With the sun turning cars into bake-ovens, and only a trickle of vehicles allowed through?

'Did you know you were doing ninety-five miles an hour, sir?'

If there had been a way out at all he would have taken it – a U-turn or whatever. But no, he'd been jammed in fore and aft, and on either side: no escape had been possible. A few yards on. A few yards on. And a woman fainting in the car next door to him. Was it any wonder that when at last he was through he had stepped down hard on the frigging pedal?

And the sods had been waiting for just that! At once, their stupid siren was blaring behind him. Nearly, so nearly, he'd kept on going, trod down harder, lost the bastards . . .

Then, thank the lord, common sense had intervened, he'd slowed, pulled over to the hard shoulder.

'I must ask you, if you will, to breathe into this.'

Well, he hadn't had a drink since yesterday evening. The sod looked disappointed when he saw the reading and handed the instrument to his mate to stash away.

'This time I'm just going to warn you, sir. You were driving much too fast. I know it can be a temptation, with a car like this, but the law is there to be obeyed.'

'I'm sorry, officer . . . it was that jam.'

'I understand, but that's no excuse. If you are wise you will accept this warning and keep your speed down in future. Is that understood?'

Yes, he bloody understood it!

'In that case you are free to go on your way.'

As a gap occurred and he pulled away he could feel his heart pounding. How could he have been such an arse? He should never have dropped his guard for a moment! Now they knew, they could place him here, driving north up the A1 . . . they had taken down his particulars! All it needed was a flash on their rotten computer . . . He drove in a manner of trance, sitting behind a truck that was doing barely sixty. What could he do? Where go? Somehow, he'd got to shake them off again!

The M of the A1 ended at a roundabout, beyond which services were signalled. He slowed, pulled in, parked, pushed through swing doors into the restaurant.

'A coffee . . . and do you have any maps here?'

'We've only got our own map.'

'That'll do.'

He took a copy to a table, sat down, spread it out, tried to grasp what it was showing him. His coffee came.

'Miss . . . can you show me where we are now?'

She pointed it out. He latched on to it eagerly, traced the A1 on its stupid route north. East . . . West? The map wasn't very helpful, was intended only to locate the positions of the company's other establishments. York perhaps . . .? But he didn't want towns! Sod Knaresborough, Leeds and all the rest. Somewhere quiet, off the main drag, where they only saw police cars once in a blue moon . . . And then he spotted it: a wriggling A road, wandering west to . . . where was it going? He scowled at the map unbelievingly. West, to where all those years ago . . .! Could it be? He folded the map, drank up coffee that was going cold. A bloody sign, it had to be – dad's road! In his bowels, he felt it could be no other . . .

'How much is this, then?'

'Oh, it's free!'

He carried it back to the car like a sacred token. Suddenly he felt he wasn't quite alone any more, a helpless fugitive, running, running . . . Dad, he would have understood. He could have talked to him, told him everything. It might even be that he was somewhere here now, watching him, guiding him, keeping him safe . . . Yes, it was possible! He could see that sad face, the kindly eyes, hear the gentle voice. My son ... And why not? He sat a while in the car before moving off ...

Now he stuck to an idle sixty, letting the Fords and Volvos rush by him. The urgency had faded, it didn't matter, he knew now just where he was going. He was on the road, dad's road. he could arrive where it led today, tomorrow. Nothing could happen to him. Dad was with him. Whatever was going on back there, he was safe ...

Almost, he could see that old car ahead of him, kingfisher blue with black trim ... the row of heads, himself and his sisters ... mum, watching out for the next loo ...

All he had to do was keep his bloody cool and drive the Jag like the slow bastards he was following ...

It had tried his patience, all the same, before he arrived at the turn-off the map had shown him. He had met with cars that seemed content with the ambling fifties and which he couldn't help but overtake. And then the taste for speed had been reborn – there was so much road stretching ahead! And he'd stayed in the fast lane for miles at a time, showing his tail to one or two who were chasing him. But then caution had returned. At the next long gap he had flashed and tucked himself back with the crawlers. And so it had gone on, mile after sodding mile, along a road that got ever more boring.

But finally, when he'd almost given up on it, the turn-off did arrive, and at once he was launched into a different world, found himself drifting along a country road. The exchange was almost a shock, so suddenly was the maelstrom of traffic left behind him! In the first mile he met only one other car and passed a single cyclist, who dismounted to give him way. A different world ... hills were rising about him, quite unlike the ones at home. Hills high, hills shapely, some of them purpled with rashes of heather. The Dales: that's where he was! And what so-and-so was going to look for him here?

He came soon to a small town, but he didn't hang about there. A few more miles and he was really amongst it, with

101

hills hemming him in on either hand. Was he far enough yet? He passed stone-built villages, crossed a river by a dainty little bridge. Perhaps the next one . . . yes! It turned out to be a village overlooked by the ruins of an ancient castle. There he spotted a likely-looking pub, parked the Jag and went on in.

'A pint!'

'You're nearly too late, chum!'

But the man reached for a glass just the same. In the bar were only two other customers, each with a half-empty glass beside him. A cool, dim room with a brick floor and wooden settles around the walls. China decorated a shelf above the counter, framed hunting prints hung here and there.

'Have you come far?'

'A . . . few miles. Any chance of some nosh?'

'Fix you a sandwich, chum, that's all. The cook goes on strike at half-two.'

'That'll do me.'

'Cheese suit you?'

'Make it two while you're at it.'

He took a long pull at his glass, then parked his backside on one of the settles. A quiet place! Outside in the street not a vehicle was stirring. The through-road passed the village by, left the wide street to its peace. Over stone tiles opposite one saw the tops of distant hills . . .

'On holiday then, are you?'

He jerked round to stare at the man who had addressed him. An elderly bloke with a wisp of beard, dressed in a sports shirt and check trousers.

'What about it?'

'Just asking! I could hear you don't belong in these parts. Let me guess now . . . if anyone asked me, I'd say you came from Suffolk way.'

He could have crowned the sod! 'And if I do?'

'No offence, my old son! Just that I was down there during the war, and my wife, she's Suffolk too. So what part are you from?

102

'Who . . . wants to know?'

'Look, don't carry on! Just a civil question. The wife, she's a Wolmering girl and I was wondering if you come from that way, too.'

Was it possible? He clung to his glass, scowling at the fellow without meeting his eyes. Something he'd have to say . . . but bloody what? He threw back a savage gulp.

'Norwich . . . I come from that way.'

'Oh, Norwich! I know Norwich. Which part?'

'Well . . . Trowse.'

'Yes, I know Trowse. It's on the road going in. So you'd know Wolmering?'

His glass was in danger! 'I've been there. Once or twice.'

'Yes . . . nice little place, isn't it? I met my wife there in 'forty-three. Her father kept the King's Head there and we met at a dance at that hall off The Street – what do they call it?'

Wicks shook his head.

'It'll come to me in a moment. But of course, it's a long time ago now and I dare say the old place has changed a bit . . .'

How could it have happened – how? In a dump off the sodding track like this! He longed to jump up and get to hell out of there, but that would only make it worse. No. Bloody no. He would have to sit it out. But any idea of holeing-up here . . .

His sandwiches came. He tried to eat them calmly, eking them out with the remains of his pint. Act normal! But the oldie and his mate were still watching him with curious eyes.

'Came up on the A1, did you?'

He grunted something.

'They're saying that jam there is worse than ever. Did it hold you up long?'

Couldn't they bloody understand – let him eat his nosh in peace? It was after hours, the pub should have been closed, yet still they sat on there, with their glasses empty . . .

'Well . . . suppose we'd better make a move, Reg.'

103

'Otherwise the missus will be wondering ... cheerio, Walter! See you this evening.'

'See you, Reg. Watch how you go!'

Then they nodded to him, a little uncertainly, and followed each other into the street. Sod them, sod them. Sod everything! He bolted the last bit of his sandwich, drained the dregs of his pint.

'How much do I owe you?'

'That's three seventy-five, mate.'

He paid. He went. He got back in the Jag. Christ, and to think – ! So where the hell could he go? He spun the Jag round in a U-turn and heard the tyres squeal as he belted away ...

Act normal. Act lousy, sodding normal. But did he know what normal was any longer? That pair were probably talking about him now, about the odd bloke from down Wolmering way. They would remember him, oh yes! And if the police got around to asking ... Suddenly those hills were no longer a sanctuary, the picturesque villages no refuge. Not them nor any rotten place ... he could drive the Jag into the ground! Here or wherever, he was a fugitive and every last hand was against him. He could look for no mercy, no friend. In the end, wouldn't he have to give himself up?

But – not just yet! While there was a chance, he was going to ride it. And, as yet, if the police were looking anywhere, it was down in Torquay and not up here. They would get round to it, they always did, but as yet they couldn't be looking for him here ... might not even be looking for him at all, if that traveller had had nothing to tell them. So? So. Keep your wool on, Wicko! You aren't a dead man yet. That stupid fifty turning up might alert them, but that was the size of it, they couldn't pin it on him ...

The fear began to dull again as he drove, mechanically holding his speed at a low level, drifting the Jag westward, westward, every mile a mile further away. Dad's road ... he felt sure of it! Along this way they had gone, through these

104

villages asleep in the sun, the windings by streams, by rocks, by falls. Somewhere here they had pulled in to picnic: he remembered a stream, the shade of trees ... Gweny, being scolded for getting her feet wet, himself being scratched by a droopy bramble. Surely, surely here there was safety, where such memories of innocence clung ...? He could feel it enclosing him, assuring him, stilling the panic that had assailed him.

Yes, there must be safety here! Only stick to these places where dad had taken them ...

By late afternoon he was entering a small town, not much more than an overgrown village. He tried to persuade himself that he remembered it, the crooked street, the rectangular market-place. Here ...? Why not! He must at least have been through it, crammed in the back with his sisters: his eyes must have rested on those same buildings, perhaps noticed the shapes of the hills surrounding them ... Today, the market-place was used only as a car-park, and behind it rose the front of a hotel. He turned into the parking. His decision was made! Bag in hand, he went in.

'A room for tonight? Certainly, sir ... would you prefer one *en suite*?'

Like the town, it was a modest establishment, but grandeur was not what he was seeking. The bedroom had an outlook towards the hills, towards a lonely road that climbed among them. It contained a television. He paused to stare at it, but then deliberately turned away. No. No! He wanted none of it: let it go on – he didn't want to know! He went down to the bar.

'A pint of Webster's, sir ...?'

He took his drink to a seat in a corner. It was the hour before dinner and there were quite a few customers in the bar. Some of them were locals, some guests, but he wanted nothing to do with either – just to sit unnoticed in his corner, putting down a couple of drinks! So he drank, and kept his eyes averted, or stared out of the window at passers-by.

But ... it wasn't to last.

105

'On your own then, are you?'

He smelt her cheap scent as she sat down beside him. A tart on the prowl! Her black dress barely reached as far as the top of her leggings.

'I thought you looked lonely, sweetheart. Told myself I'd come and cheer you up. I'm Kylie, they know me here. If you're buying another drink I wouldn't half like one.'

Why didn't he tell her to go to hell? He wasn't in the mood for sodding tarts! There was one back there . . . And this one looked ancient, had to be thirty-five at least. He liked them young, in their teens for preference. So why didn't he tell her . . .?

'What's it to be?'

'Gin and tonic. Are you eating here, sweetheart?'

'I've got a room here.'

'I thought you might have. Perhaps we can – you know! – brighten it up for you.'

'I didn't say that . . .!'

'You didn't have to. But look, we can talk about it later.'

He fetched the drinks. She edged up close to him. Nobody seemed to be taking much notice. Yet she was only too plainly a tart in her see-through dress and patterned leggings.

'What's your name, sweetheart?'

'Just call me Kenny.'

'What do you do for a living, Kenny?'

'That's my business!'

'All right, all right! I can see you're making a good thing of it, lover. That wouldn't be your Jag out there, would it?'

'Suppose it is?'

'Ooh la! Let me guess. You're a rep for one of the big breweries. Would it be Bass, now, or Whitbread?'

Was it stamped in his face, his late occupation? He scowled at the window. Next, she too would be guessing . . . He fought down the emotions that tangled within him, took a pull from his glass. Perhaps she was what he needed just now . . .

'We could go for a drive, lover. I've never been in a Jag. And I know some good places. What about it?'

'We'll see.'

'After we've had some grub, of course, we can't let you starve. Is it on?'

'First, let's bloody eat!'

'That's my man! They've got grouse on tonight. Do you fancy grouse?'

'Any damn thing!'

'Oooh ... he is in a way!' She leaned against him. 'But we can take care of that, can't we, lover-boy? Kylie knows the business, never you fear. Shall we go in?'

He drank up. Still he wasn't certain if he wanted to go through with it. He didn't fancy her. She was the tall, slim type, the sort that never much turned him on. But she had a way with her, a mateyness, he could feel himself softening a little towards her. He let her lead him into the dining-room and to a table by itself, in an alcove. They sat. She slid him a sly smile.

'Got a missus, have we, Kenny?'

'No ... I'm not married.'

'It makes a change. Half the blokes I see here are on the run from their wives. I thought maybe – the mood you're in! But perhaps you've just had a hard day. Have you come far?'

'From ... down south.'

'Oh, I could tell that's where you came from. Anywhere I know?'

'Let's just bloody eat!'

'Well, if you don't want to talk about it! But there's no need to be mysterious with me, I never breathe a word about my clients. Some of them just want to talk. You can let your hair down with Kylie.'

He stared at her. But just then the waiter approached them with the menu, and he grabbed it thankfully, made an act of going through the dishes on offer.

'Some wine, sir ... perhaps the Beaujolais?'

'Oh yes please – shall we, Kenny?'

'Well . . .'

'That's my man! And bring it to us straight away.'

The waiter left; and almost at once a second waiter fetched them the wine. When it was poured she raised her glass, with a twinkle in her eye.

'Cheers, lover-boy . . . now you can relax! So what was it you were going to tell Kylie?'

'What makes you think . . .?'

'Oh, come on! I'm not a beginner at this game.'

'But . . .'

'Well, it's up to you. I'm here to give value for money, old sourpuss.'

He drank wine. Hell and hell, it was almost on the tip of his tongue! For an instant he was sensing the relief waiting to flood through him if only he dared . . . But no, he mustn't. No! At the most, a hint was all he dared give. A hint that somewhere behind him . . . back there, in far-off Suffolk . . . He drank again.

'All right, then! Say I've had a bit of trouble back home!'

'Woman trouble?'

'Bloody no! Just something I don't want to think about.'

'Not trouble with the law?'

He drank. 'Could be. Oh, don't worry! They aren't looking for me.'

'Trouble with a bloke, then?'

'Yes. With a bloke.'

'You – hurt him much?'

He just drank.

'Well . . . old Kenny!' She drank too. She shook her head. 'I'll never understand it! The way men carry on. But there you are. I suppose it's what being men is all about. And now you're fed up?'

'Bloody fed up.'

'And you came up here to get away from it.'

'Something like that.'

She nodded: stared with a look half curious, half compassionate. 'Were you . . . drunk?'

'Perhaps . . . a sodding hangover.'

'Want to tell me what happened?'

He stared at his glass. 'Let's just say I met a bloke at the wrong moment. I didn't know the sod from Adam, he was just . . . well, never mind! It was a bit of bad luck, that's all. And now I want to bloody forget it.'

'It's all over, is it?'

'Yes. All over.'

'You won't have to meet him when you go back?'

'No . . . I won't.'

She tipped her glass. 'Then cheer up, you soft sod! You've got me here to forget it with, and Johnny is just going to bring our nosh. What's so sad about that? Go on, see if you can give me a smile!'

'Perhaps . . .'

'Go on!'

And somehow he managed it . . . when was the last time he smiled?

The food was good and he had eaten only sandwiches since breakfast that morning at the Little Chef. Soup, the grouse and Black Forest gâteau, helped along with plentiful wine. He did it justice, felt almost too full . . . were things really as desperate as he'd thought them? He found himself smiling again without effort when she handed him his coffee and mints. While, for afters . . .?

'We can go to your room, Kenny. Nobody here is going to notice.'

'You wanted a ride . . .'

'That was before. Now you'll have trouble keeping me awake.'

She scrubbed out the cigarette she had lit and he left a fiver on the table. She was right, nobody paid any attention as they passed up the stairs together. In the bedroom she fitted herself to him and gave him a long, lingering, compelling kiss, then pushed him away and stripped off. And yes . . . she did know the business.

'What's the usual . . .?'

'Up to you, lover-boy.'

He peeled off five tens.

'Are you coming down? There's still time for a drink.'

'No . . . not after that!'

'You're kidding, my lad!'

She went. He lay a while on the bed, then his eyes strayed to the TV. Should he? He glanced at his watch: they were only ten minutes into the news. Finally he got up and switched it on – bloody Ireland was what they were on about! – and sat watching, item by item, until the weather forecast took over. Could he have missed it . . .? But that seemed unlikely. It would scarcely have figured in the early slots. A brief mention before the weather was all that ITV was likely to have given it. He stabbed the switch. So . . . nothing! That sodding traveller must have been a frost. Torquay police weren't looking for him and he could accept the composure the tart had left him with . . .

He donned his pyjamas, got into bed and lay awake for a very little while. Perhaps . . . perhaps. His last waking thought was of the Super Minx and of his father driving it . . .

8

He slept well and awoke with a strange feeling of remoteness.
All that, the events of yesterday . . . hadn't they happened a
great while ago? In the first moments of waking, it seemed so.
He appeared to have crossed an invisible frontier. He lay,
blankly gazing through the window at the cleft in the hills
and its lonely little road. Beyond, he had gone beyond! Up
here the bastards couldn't reach him. Almost, he might be
here on some sort of holiday, just like before with dad and the
others . . . No police, no Lord Muck, no scolding mum. Just . . .

Hold on to that: hold on to it!

He jumped out of bed and went to take his shower. When
he emerged he found a tea-tray waiting and with it the
morning papers he had ordered. He leafed through them
impatiently, confident that nothing awaited him there. But . . .
he was wrong. In a corner of one of them, his eye lit on an
obscure paragraph. SUFFOLK TRAGEDY – MAN RELEASED. It
consisted of no more than half a dozen lines: he sat down to
read them. The bloody sods . . . they'd let the frigging traveller
go!

They'd let him go! What did it mean? He sat scowling at
the item for minutes. Had they put it in deliberately, guessing
that he was going to see it? If they'd let him go . . . He must
have told them something, something that put him in the
clear, something . . . But bloody what? What else could it have
been . . .?

He read the paragraph a dozen times, seeking for the hint
that wasn't there. No, they were too clever for that! They just

wanted to leave him in the air. They had got something on him, that was the message, they had bloody Wicko in their sights. He flung the paper from him . . . sod them! And just when he was feeling that he'd put it behind him . . .

Then he grabbed the paper back again – because wasn't it still possible that he was reading too much into it? Bloody yes! They had made no mention of following other lines of enquiry. The man who had been assisting them had been released . . . between the lines, they'd got nothing vital out of him. He had told his tale and the tale had stood up: that was the long and short of the item. Well . . . wasn't it?

He drank cold tea. So he had let it shake him up . . . but there was no real cause for it. All along, the odds had been that the traveller, after giving his statement, would be allowed on his way. Nothing new or unexpected had happened. Nothing to say he was in any deeper. So bloody so . . . He gulped tea, slung the paper, began to pull on his clothes. No more panic . . . keep acting normal! Bloody Wicko on one of his trips . . .

'Will you want the room for tonight, sir?'

He hesitated. Last night he'd had that in mind. But perhaps he had said too much to the tart, and she would surely be around again . . .

'No. Bring me my bill.'

'If you'll pay at the desk, sir . . .'

Yes: he would be better off out of there. On the road again, going west: on the track of the Super Minx still . . .

From a newsagent's he bought a proper map, one that showed all the roads, big and little. Back in the Jag he spread it over the wheel and frowningly traced a course with his finger. He knew just where he was going now, to that town in the Lakes where dad had taken them, a town where mountains had huddled round them and one of the big lakes had stretched almost from their doorstep. He found it: the name he knew from often having heard his sisters mention it; but the way there was less than straightforward, involving some lesser roads and vital junctions. Well, dad had found it and so would he! Only now there was another problem creeping up on him, one he never thought would ever trouble him again . . . yes! He was running short of money – him: Wicko: the jackpot cowboy!

It had struck him first when he paid off the tart – if he ran out of cash, where the hell could he go for some? He had his cards and his cheque-book, of course, but using these would put him right on the spot. Like as not they would have a call out, just waiting for Wicko to make such a move. They could trace him from bank to cashpoint, nail him down, drop a hand on his shoulder . . .

He checked his wallet. After paying the hotel bill, he had barely two hundred left – now he was regretting those lousy fifties he had made away with in his grate! They might have been traced, but that was unlikely, and with them in hand he would have been laughing. He'd been a fool, reacting like that – why hadn't he thought? But he sodding hadn't . . .

Irritably he stuffed the wallet away again. If it came to it, he would just have to keep on running. Use a cashpoint, write a cheque, then get back on the road again. So, in the end, they might catch him – but he'd give them a run for their money first! He backed the Jag out of the parking and set it on the course the map had pointed out to him . . .

He would have driven fast if he could, but the nature of the road prevented it. For mile on mile it wriggled its way by moorland, rock and village street. But, slowly, patience grew with him again. He began to let the Jag dawdle. Because he wasn't in any sodding hurry, was he, didn't have to be there at a set time? Dad hadn't raced when he came this way . . . for one thing, mum wouldn't have let him! And dad had done the whole trip in one day, from Suffolk right across to the Lakes. They had been up before daybreak, he remembered that, with the stars still in the sky – August it had been, like it was now, and just as hot later on. The girls had been wearing their summer dresses, with him in short pants and a cotton shirt ... yes, it was all coming back to him! And why not, when he was driving this road ...? Couldn't he pretend, just for a little while: pretend he was only here because ...?

Defiantly, on the hour, he switched on the radio for the news. No mention! He switched it off again and let his mind wander back to those memories. Dad had worn a hat, but not the old trilby that still hung in the hall ... no, he seemed to remember a smart straw with a green ribbon and a feather stuck in it. And mum ...? Mum he couldn't bring to mind! Perhaps that bonnet she was so fond of ... and he, they'd given him a cap of some sort, which he loathed, and used to throw at the girls ... And he had taken his teddy. There had been a fuss about that, but never mind – he'd still taken it! And somehow it had all worked out and, tired to death, they had arrived at their boarding-house – would he remember that too? It was one of a terrace, overlooking the lake ...

He had to stop the consult the map and pulled over at a pub that stood alone at the junction. They were serving coffee, so he went in and found a table on which to spread the map. The publican fetched him his cup and lingered.

'So where would you be off to, then?'

Couldn't any of the sods round here mind their business? He gave the man his best scowl.

'If it's the A66 you're after ...'

'I can read a bloody map, thank you!'

'Oh, all right! If you feel like that ...'

The fellow gave him a hard stare before he shrugged and moved away. Wicks drank his coffee. Sod everything! But the bastard shouldn't have been so nosy ...

He laid money on the table, seized the map and got out of there. Once more he'd left someone remembering him and who, if the police got on his trail ...

'Here ... you left your change!'

'Keep it!'

'I don't want your bloody money!'

'Just ... keep it!'

He gunned the Jag and sent it squealing out of the forecourt.

But then he had to brake hard to negotiate the junction – oh yes, that sod wasn't going to forget him!

He drove on, seething, and perhaps it was fortunate that the A road was only another few miles ahead. Came a slip-road, came the duals, and then he could really let the Jag motor! Bloody police were there? Let them chase him! A hundred and ten ... a hundred and twenty. Bloody horns blaring. Sods flashing him. Out of the way – Wicko's coming! It was mad, stupid, and he knew it, but a black rage was driving him on. He had to get it out of his system, take it out on the sodding road ...

It was a roundabout that finally checked him and cut him down to the level of common traffic. There he had to queue and wait, make sure of his direction from the signs. It gave him pause, a space to catch up. Perhaps – perhaps, when he got across there! His mind was dizzy, couldn't think, he could only scowl at the car ahead ...

When his turn came, he took it mechanically, and let the Jag drift with the vehicles around him. Dully he noticed hills rising ahead ... hills that were more than hills: bloody mountains! He was nearly there. He let the Jag drift still. And now the cars were hooting him to get a move on ... He didn't give a frig about that either, just went at his own pace. Let them wait. For Wicko.

'You can try the hotels, of course, but I'm sorry. This is August.'

He had found the terrace, it might have been the very house, but in every window the sign was the same: No Vacancies. The same terrace: in point of fact, it was further from the lake than he remembered. In between were a garage and a couple of houses, while a camp-site occupied the lake shore. But ... the same terrace! He had recognized it at once, the rather drab row of Victorian bow-fronts, the steps that once he had played on, the iron rails, the pots of ferns ... Across the road dad had parked the car, where now there

115

wasn't a single vacant space. No bloody vacancies, one side or the other! He'd had to park the Jag with its wheels on the pavement.

'I'm afraid it's always the same at this time of year. Unless you book, there isn't a chance. But like I say, you can try the hotels.'

'When I was a kid . . . it was a long time ago . . .'

'Yes, I know. People are always coming back. I really would help you if I could, but I'm very sorry. We're quite full up.'

'And nowhere else along here . . .?'

The woman shook her head. 'I can save you the trouble. You'll have to try elsewhere.'

He got back in the Jag and sat staring. And this was the bloody sanctuary he'd run to! A sodding town so jam-full of visitors that like as not he would have to sleep in the car. The hotels, she'd said, oh yes! Where a couple of nights would skin him. Where he daren't write a cheque or flash his card, or even enter his own name in the book. Last night he'd been Smith, but then he'd paid cash. Well, the end of that game wasn't far away . . . He hugged the wheel. And when he was skint? Stuck here, bloody hundreds of miles from everything . . .?

'You do realize, sir . . .'

'I know!'

He set the Jag rolling and drove off the pavement. Even the rotten parking . . .! He cruised it down to the camp-site, where a bit of worn verge let him get off the road. Like everywhere else it was packed, a litter of tents, caravans and caravettes. People in shorts came and went, children romped, kicked their balls. Sodding holiday people, while he . . .! Was there any point in him hanging on? Better to pack the game in now and clear off home while he could still afford the petrol . . .

He stared at the lake, at the mountains. If he could only be sure of what was happening back there . . . Two days it was now, two lousy days, and bloody something must be going on. They'd released the traveller, he had told his tale, they'd let him go back to his stupid van . . . and it rested with him,

116

there was no one else, not a single soul who could hang it on Wicko! They'd found the note, of course, but it wasn't proof, nor his silly conversation with Sandra. No: it rested with the gypo. Unless the gypo could nail him there wasn't a case that would stand up . . .

He wrestled with the wheel: so, couldn't he find out – say, put a call through to Gweny or mum? He didn't have to ask them outright, just let it come up as they were having their chat. Oh . . . about that job in the forest, have they got any further with that? Was it the gypo? No, I hadn't heard! You mean to say they let him go? And then they would tell him . . . only, what would they tell him? That Lord Muck was wanting a word with him? He slammed his hands down on the wheel! No. Frigging no! He couldn't do it.

Then . . . someone else? Sid? Biker? But he didn't know their phone numbers. And ten to one they would smell something, perhaps even report it to the police.

So . . . no and no again.

He would just have to carry on.

And in the end, if it came to it, he'd take the risk and draw some money . . .

Sitting there he nearly missed the news and jabbed it on at the last moment. But he needn't have bothered. The only crime they had time for was a bank robbery in the home counties.

Meanwhile he needed his rotten lunch and a place to spend the night . . . somewhere, anywhere!

He set the Jag rolling again.

'A room for tonight? Well, it just happens . . .'

At another time, he wouldn't have looked at the joint – an unpromising pub on a corner on the outskirts of the town. But it offered food and it had parking, a yard where he could shove the Jag, so he had gone in, ordered a pint and chosen a dish from the chalked menu. And then, just on the off-chance . . .

'I've had a bloke let me down. It isn't the Ritz, but we'll make you comfortable and you can have it for twenty quid. Does that suit?'

'It . . . suits.'

'I can tell you, mate, you're lucky. It's likely the only room in town. That's the way it gets here in August.'

First he ate, then he lugged his bag up to a room that wasn't much larger than a cupboard. But it was a room, a cheap room, and he was told he could have it for the rest of the week. Its single window looked down on the yard and on the Jag among its plebeian neighbours, while by craning his neck a little he could just get a glimpse of a sunlit peak above the roofs. Well . . . he wasn't here for the view! A roof and a bed were all he needed. His mouth twisted bitterly as he surveyed it: Wicko's pad. While in the lousy bank . . .

'Will it do you, mate?'

'Bloody have to, won't it?'

He'd gone back to the bar for another pint. The place was crowded, yokels mostly. A game of darts was in progress at the other end.

'Come far today?'

Did he have to ask that? At the end of the counter stood a phone. He stared at it for a moment, and then away. He drank.

'On business, are you? You can phone from here.'

'Perhaps later . . .'

'If you want to be private . . .'

'Later will do!'

'Right you are. It'll be quieter in here then.'

He turned his back on the counter. Of course the fellow was curious. His clothes, the Jag, his swish bag . . . and then for him to rent that hole upstairs! Even at a pinch in crowded August it must be making the bloke wonder – there had to be a hotel somewhere that could have squeezed him in, if he'd tried. He drank up.

'Give me another!'

All about him the customers were working people, labour-

118

ers, mechanics, shop-assistants: he stood out like a sore thumb. And yet once, and not so long ago . . . often still dressed in his overalls. And, like them, with a job to go back to, mates to greet, a foreman to cheek . . .

'Here we are, mate. One fifty. I was thinking, will you want the room after tonight?'

'I'll . . . let you know.'

'I mean, if you tried . . .'

He stood out too far: the sod didn't want him!

'I'll see.'

'Well, of course, you're welcome. But I know that room is a bit of a dug-out.'

'It will do. For tonight.'

'There you are. But don't think I will take offence . . .'

Somehow he controlled himself, went on taking pulls at his glass. It was no use, he had to knuckle under, this was his hole and he daren't foul it. Until . . . until . . . Until bloody what? The glass was empty again before he knew it. He slammed it down.

'See you, then!'

'If you're late in, just give us a ring!'

Outside he strode away, he didn't care where, let the town and its crowded streets swallow him. In the pub, out there, wherever, he was alone, a frigging outcast. He couldn't talk to people. He didn't want to. Didn't want even to catch their eye. Just to be alone, like he sodding was . . . alone, alone, alone! So the streets, the people, the shop-windows went by him, and he discovered where, all along, he had been heading – back there, to that road to the lake, to the line of terrace houses that had rejected him. Yes . . . there! To that single spot where he was connected and might feel . . .

Now he was certain he had the right house, the one where he'd rung the bell. He stood devouring it with his eyes, the steps, the porch, the rails, the bow-windows. No doubt the paintwork and curtains had changed, and the sign above the door was new, but nothing else. That was the place. He could feel it in every bone. The girls had had a room at the back, but he had slept at the front with mum and dad. The room with the bow. He could remember running to the window to stare at the foreign world without, the strange hills, the great spread of water, the Super Minx down below. So different ... so improbably different! It had seemed to him like a different planet. But dad had known of it, had brought them there after all those hours of journeying ...

Later, holding dad's hand, with the girls running ahead and mum following behind, he had toddled down to the shores of that lake – had the camp-site been there then? They had been allowed to paddle, though the beach was gravel and rather painful to the feet. Then – yes! A rowing-boat. He could still feel it, the hardness, the awkwardness of the spot where he'd squatted, with Flo's firm hand on his shoulder to stop him climbing up and falling in ... Dad had rowed them to an island. They had picnicked there. The girls had run about exploring, but he had had to stay with mum. And on the beach where they'd pulled the boat up he had found curious stones, one with a hole through it ...

They had made that trip again before leaving, but for the rest it was back in the car. Dad had driven them over hairy roads, by other lakes, by waterfalls. Then ... a house, a sort of museum, but his memory of it was vague. And walks up some painfully steep paths, for no reason that he could now remember.

Another world ... Another time.

And all contained in the house across the road.

And he ...?

Another sodding being, a fugitive, a frigging question in Lord Muck's eyes!

How much longer could he take it, be what he was, stay outside?

He began to walk again, down to the camp-site. No one stopped him going in. He made his way through the tents and caravans to the edge of the lake, the gravelled beach. And he could keep walking ... why not? Into that lake of so long ago.

120

Up to his waist. Up to his chest. On and on. Till ... But he bloody didn't. He chose a spot and sat down, sat along with some other loafers; stretched himself out and lay staring at the sky, across which light skeins of cloud were drifting. Kids played around him, paddled. A bloke was launching a canoe. Snatches of conversation came to him. And bloody time drifted with the clouds.

Could he do it, if he had to?

He could feel his eyelids closing. Let them!

Perhaps an hour later he got up and walked back towards the town.

Towards the town, but not the pub: that was just to be the place where he slept. Instead, for his evening meal, he chose a modest café in the town centre. The place was crowded, it went without saying, and he was obliged to share a table, his fellow-diner a middle-aged lady who met him with a shy smile. He managed not to scowl back and made his choice from the menu. The waitress fetched his order. He sipped tea and ate.

'Another lovely day we've had ...'

She was going to talk, she couldn't help it. A plumpish woman with dyed hair, ear-rings and a wart on her chin. He nodded vaguely, went on eating.

'Am I right in thinking you are a visitor?'

He nodded again.

'Forgive my curiosity! But are you alone? I have a reason for asking.'

'I'm ... alone.'

'Then you might be interested. I'm a member of the Towns-women's Guild. Tonight we're holding our Summer Revels, and if you have nothing better to do ...'

He gazed at her. Was she serious? She was trying to make her eyes lively! In a moment, she was fishing in her bag and coming up with a printed leaflet ...

'You see? At the Assembly Rooms. There'll be dancing on the green and everything. And a buffet supper with wine. I'm sure you'll enjoy yourself if you come.'

'I'm sorry, but . . .'

'Oh, you needn't worry about not having a partner! There will be plenty to go round. In fact, my daughter is looking for one.'

'But . . .!'

'You don't dance? Well, it isn't compulsory. And there are plenty of other things for you to do . . .'

In another moment he would have thrown his plate at her, but she must have caught something in the look he was giving her. With a little nervous movement she pushed the leaflet across to him, then gathered her bag and rose from the table.

'Well, if you should change your mind! We're beginning at half-past seven . . .'

Sod the bitch. Sod her! He stared after her malignly. Didn't she know, couldn't she tell . . .? He felt the itch in his fingers as he watched her leave. But at once another customer was taking her seat, a lean, grey-haired bloke, who also smiled at him.

'This seat isn't taken, is it . . .?'

He ate savagely, dismissively. He had to frigging eat, but why? Why? All he asked them to do was to let him alone! The bloke had a paper which he was rustling and glancing through: an evening edition, with a stop-press column . . .

'England did all right, then.'

'England . . .?'

'They finished on 342. Then they took two wickets before stumps. I'd say they were in with a chance, wouldn't you?'

He held himself tight. Tighter. 'Could I look at your paper when you've finished with it?'

'Help yourself, old boy!'

The man passed it across to him, turned his attention to the waitress.

Wicks made a pretence of leafing through it, but the stop-press was what he was after. And – bloody yes! – it was there,

122

a few lines headed: THE SUFFOLK TRAGEDY. 'The Suffolk Police, who yesterday released a man they had been questioning, said today that another man was helping with their enquiries. As yet he has not been named, but the police are confident that progress has been made. The body of the victim has yet to be identified.'

Another frigging man . . . But who? Who?

'A pity about Tufnell, don't you think?'

'Tufnell . . .?'

'Well, it isn't often that a tail-ender comes so close to a century!'

Stuff bloody Tufnell! He handed the paper back, trying to keep his hand from trembling. Who? And what had he told them? Surely they hadn't come up with some bastard . . .

'Are you all right, laddie?'

'What . . .? Yes!'

'It is a little close in here. Perhaps . . .'

'I'm bloody all right!'

The man shook his head, took up the paper again.

Wicks paid and went. Who? Who? Clearly the sod must have told them something! And it was a bloke, not the tart – as yet frigging Sandra hadn't been mentioned! So . . .? He was shaking, he couldn't help it. Had some other devil been around there? Out of sight, say, in the trees, a witness to . . . how much had the bastard seen? And yet, yet – why hadn't he come forward, if what he'd seen . . . why? Why wait till the police picked him up? Could he have been on some game of his own . . .?

He wanted to be sick: the meal he had just eaten was grumbling in his stomach. Those few bloody lines in a paper had thrust him right back there, into the forest. Alone, they'd been alone, or it couldn't have happened, he could never have done what he did. He could see the bristly face before him, the greedy eyes, the reaching hand. And then . . . then . . . He could feel his hands jerking! And the bloody eyes growing wider . . . Wider! Bloodshot, rheumy eyes growing wider. And suddenly glazing . . .

123

If someone had been there, could they have stayed silent, gone on lurking in the gloomy pines – watched him drag that burden to the tank, wrench back the netting, dump it in, and still say nothing? It couldn't have been – didn't make sense! Even a bloody poacher would have run to the police, at least have given them a hint of what they'd find there in the tank . . .

So . . . what could the bugger have seen? Seen him picking up the money afterwards – all except that rotten note that somehow had gone in the tank with the old bloke? Perhaps not even that – just a sighting of the Jag coming or going – someone's Jag, he'd hardly have taken the number! – driven by some bloke he probably couldn't describe . . .

But then, why hadn't he come forward sooner? A poacher or some such sod he must be! A bloody delinquent, whose word . . . Wouldn't there be an out for him in that?

Yes. Yes. A chance there must still be.

So why was he trembling like a frigging leaf?

Because, because he couldn't bloody help it!

He'd got shoved back there, back in the forest . . .

The lake was in front of him. He shuddered, turned from it. What he needed now was a sodding drink. Even though he spewed his lousy guts up . . .

Once more, he aimed his steps back into the town.

He didn't spew his guts up. The first pint settled them and he took it on from there: pint after bloody pint. What was the point of keeping count?

'You're pushing the boat out, aren't you, mate . . .?'

He had chosen a pub in one of the back streets, not the one where he'd booked for the night but another of a similar character. A working-class pub, like the ones that till recently . . . not a pub like the sodding Bell! Here, he was rubbing shoulders with his kind, his mates, the sort who could understand. He leered at a tart, who leered back: but he wasn't after that either. Drink up, bloody Wicko!

'Out here on a trip, mate?'

'Just for a frigging change of scene.'

'Thought you might be. Come far?'

'Down bloody south. The other side.'

'What's the beer like where you come from?'

'We get Webster's down there too.'

'Can't beat it, mate. Not Webster's.'

'Drink up, and have one on me . . .'

That tart again . . . she kept leering! He'd seen worse, and seen better. Sitting there drinking in with a real roughneck . . . there, again! He winked back . . .

'Sure you need another?'

'Bloody fill it up!'

'Well, I hope you aren't driving, mate! Are you sure?'

'Just fill the bugger.'

'If I were you, I'd make this my last . . .'

When he lurched outside it was dark and the ill-lit street deserted. And he hadn't got bloody far when he felt a hand on his shoulder.

'A word in your ear, matey!'

It was the sodding roughneck who had been with the tart. He spun Wicks round, held him by the arm, thrust his face close to Wicks's.

'I don't know what your game was in there, but that bloody girl belongs to me. So just don't go getting any ideas, or you'll know who you have to deal with . . .'

And his hands were there, round the bugger's neck . . .

Well, the sod had asked for it, hadn't he? Was struggling, still bloody asking for it, trying to pull Wicko's hands away . . .

Had he done for him? He didn't know, never meant to bloody-well know! Just left the sod propped against the wall, wheezing and groaning . . . no, he hadn't done for him!

'You – you're in a fine way, aren't you?'

He had to be helped up the stairs to his room. There he collapsed on the bed, lay panting, staring at the ceiling. He was seeing that face again, the bristly face, and the eyes . . . the eyes.

125

Up there, on the frigging ceiling!

Weren't those eyes ever going away . . .?

'Do you reckon it's safe to leave you, then? I don't want you being sick all over the bed.'

'Yes . . . I'll be . . .'

'I'll look in again. Though why you had to get yourself in a state like this . . .'

A door closed. He could still see the face.

But in the end, he must have slept.

9

When he woke he woke suddenly, his eyes staring at sunlight on a patch of wall. His head throbbed and his rancid mouth felt so gummed-up that it was difficult to swallow. His limbs too: they seemed paralysed, as though he were never going to move them again: he lay helplessly gazing at the sunlit wall, trying to connect with what he was seeing.

He had slept, he had dreamed, and the dream was still with him, almost as real as the bedroom wall . . . faces, faces that watched him: the faces of dad, mum and the girls. They were grouped together on the shore of the island, picnic-island on the lake, watching him, calling to him, Gweny waving him to join them. Only . . . he couldn't do that. He was in the rowing-boat and the oars were too big for him to manage. He had got one of them stuck in a rowlock, but no way could he make it row. He tried and tried, but it was no use, he couldn't get the blade into the water . . . it worked for dad, but not for him. The boat went on drifting, drifting further away . . .

He scowled and scowled at the painful sunlight. Was it something that had really happened – a mishap of his child-hood, come back to him now as a dream? He racked his throbbing brain for a trace of such a memory, but nothing came. Yet, if it had happened, was it possible that he would have entirely forgotten it . . .?

A tap on the door made him wince: the landlord's beefy face peered round it.

'You're awake, then! I just wondered . . . it's gone nine and I didn't hear you stirring. Feeling rough, are you?'

He winced again. The fellow gave him a wink. 'Last night you were pretty near legless! But I dare say you don't remember much about that.'

Did he? There was something . . . something . . . He dragged a hand across his forehead. The landlord was watching him with a glint of amusement in his eye.

'You were in the Nag's Head – remember now? Ted Willis was in here and told me about it. You were giving Slash Taylor's wench the eye and he followed you outside to fettle you.'

'I was . . . in a scrap?'

'I'll say you were! Slash Taylor has had enough of you, mate. Bloody near strangled him you did, they had to dose him with brandy to bring him round. And you don't remember?'

'He . . . he's all right?'

'Oh yes. He could walk home afterwards. But you, you can't know your own strength, mate. And with all those pints inside you, too!'

'I think . . .'

'Is it coming back now?'

'Something . . .'

'Well, it happens to all of us! And no harm done, or not much. Do you think you'll fancy any breakfast?'

'A sodding drink!'

'It's fruit juice for you, mate. Something to get the taste out of your mouth.'

He dragged himself from the bed and got under a shower. A tumbler of orange juice waited for him when he got back. He drank it, grimacing, but it had its effect and the pulsing began to ease from his head. So . . . no harm done! But he'd been bloody lucky to get away with that. As of now he would have to ration the booze, make certain he never got in that state again. It wasn't his fault, he hadn't picked the quarrel, but it had happened just the bloody same . . . his hands had got round that bastard's throat. He could have been another one on the account . . .

At once, the news item flashed before his eye and the knuckles of the hand that clasped the tumbler had blanched white.

'Some breakfast, then?'

'I couldn't sodding face it!'

'Will you be wanting your room tonight?'

'Yes . . . tonight. I'm off out.'

'Take my advice and you'll make an early night of it.'

The sun was too bright, the people too many, the noise of the traffic an infernal din. He kept to the shady side of streets and stared ahead: stared at nothing. The problem hadn't gone away. Back there . . . back there. He needed to know, to frigging know! Only just now his mind was in a daze, in a turmoil. He couldn't think, only keep the panic under . . .

He tried to think of mum. Of Joycey. Of Gweny, so happy in the house he had bought for her. Yes . . . that was what was back there, the place he belonged to, the people. Think of that! Joycey hadn't quite forgiven him, but she hadn't turned him down either . . . and mum was behind him. And Gweny. Together, they would surely make a go of it . . . And then the house, they would take it apart, do everything to it that Joycey wanted, everything that money could pay for . . . because, never forget his sodding millions! He might be separated from them now, but they were waiting for whenever . . . Mechanically, his hand felt for his wallet, tried to ignore the flatness it was touching . . . it was only here he was a pauper! Back home, the stuff was waiting in cart-loads . . .

For moments he held that vision in his mind, a vision of content and smiling people, and then it faded, as though a switch had been touched, and in an instant he was staring into Lord Muck's eyes. It wasn't going to happen – because the sod wouldn't let it! From the first he had seen through into Wicko's soul. The other bastards didn't count, with them one could get away with it, but not with Mucker. He bloody knew! So . . . so?

He came to a standstill in the bustle of the street. But even that swine would need to have proof, if ever he was to hang it on Wicko! Just to know was not enough, he had to make a case to persuade a jury. And if the frigging proof wasn't there . . . if it wasn't. If it wasn't! How could he bloody find out? How could he? How?

Along the street was a newsagent's shop. He went in and bought every sodding paper. Then he marched into the nearest café, by chance the one he had patronized previously.

'A black coffee – and make it strong!'

By the time it came he was through the first paper. Then the second, and the third – did none of the sods care about murder any longer? In the end it was the sixth one he tackled, and then only a repetition of last night's stop-press: an unnamed man was helping their enquiries and they were confident that progress had been made. Progress – but what bloody progress? He searched the rest of the papers in vain. Could it be a trick? Some stupid feint to put on the pressure, flush him out of his retreat?

He drank the coffee and ordered more. If it was a trick, then it was working! He couldn't go on not knowing, some hint he must have of what was going on . . . He kept sipping the coffee. They would guess, of course. There was only one source he could go to. And ten to one the phones were bugged, would nail him down the moment he opened his mouth. So, if he made that call . . . yes, it would be back on the bloody road! He would have to run. But then, at least, he needn't be afraid of drawing some dosh . . . or had they put a clamp on his account, left him with just these few shrinking notes?

'Anything else, sir . . .?'

He paid and got up to leave the table.

'Sir . . . these newspapers!'

He nearly told her what she could do with them, but didn't.

Mum – it would have to be mum: Gweny was usually out on Tuesdays. He would be in for a dressing-down, he knew, but after that, once he got her talking . . . He passed a phone box in the high street – not there! He wanted somewhere quieter. Somewhere . . . He kept walking, came at last to the road with the terrace houses. At its end was one of the old-style boxes. He went in and laid out his change.

'Mum . . .?'

For nerve-racking moments all he could hear were noises in a background, then a sudden, firm click, followed by his mother's determined voice.

'Kenny?'

'Yes, it's me, mum!'

'Oh.'

'Mum, I thought I should give you a ring!'

'I see. Well, my son, I'm not sure I want to talk to you.'

'But mum, really – !'

'Oh no, Kenny. Don't waste your time trying to get round me. I've done my best with you, Kenny, and every time you let me down. Well, this is once too often. I'm not putting up with it any more.'

'But . . . what have I done?'

'What haven't you done! And just when there was a chance of things working out. What do you think I could say to Joyce, Kenny? And her mother too. What could I tell them?'

'Mum, I couldn't help it!'

'Oh, yes. There seem a lot of things that you can't help, son.'

'I felt – I just needed to get away!'

'Yes. And you've done it once too often.'

'But it wasn't like that!'

'Ha.'

'I needed to think, mum. To . . . get myself straight.'

'And for that you needed to run off, with never a word – so that I had to ring Vera to find out where you'd gone?'

'Mum, I'm sorry, I'm really sorry. I didn't mean it to look like that. It was just . . . well, everything happening! I needed some time, time to get myself used to it. But I didn't mean . . .'

'Tell me straight, sonny. You're not living there with some loose woman?'

131

'No, I swear! It isn't like that at all. It's how I'm telling you, I needed to get away.'

'I see. And no doubt you're staying at the smartest hotel you could find.'

'No – I've got a room, a little room. A room at a pub, without even a washbasin . . .'

'And you're not in some trouble?'

'No!'

'I want the truth, sonny. Tell me.'

'Mum . . . oh, mum!'

'Well. Are you?'

'What's the use of saying it, if you won't believe me?'

'Kenny, you're mother's not a fool.'

'Oh please, mum. Please.'

He grappled with the receiver. Should he tell he about last night? A pub brawl – she would understand that! It wouldn't be the first time he'd had to confess one . . .

'Well . . . if you must know . . .'

'Go on.'

'Really, mum, it was nothing! There was this bloke in a pub last night. He thought I was eyeing up his girl.'

'And were you, Kenny?'

'No – I wasn't! It was she who kept eyeing me. But he was drunk, and when I left he came out after me and started a row. And that's all there is to it.'

'You were in a fight, then.'

'Just believe me. It was nothing!'

'You haven't changed, Kenny.'

'Oh . . . mum!'

He could almost see her shaking her head . . .

'Hang on – I've got to put in some more money!'

Luckily, he had paid with a note at the café. But the change on the box was shrinking and still they were a long way from what he needed to know. The coin clinked home.

'Mum?'

'I'm here, son. I suppose I'm lucky to have you ring me at all.'

'Mum, I'm truly sorry. I really am. I don't deserve a mum like you.'

'Sometimes I think the same, Kenny.'

'I know, I know. And then there's poor Joyce.'

'Joycey – I'm surprised you remember her! She was round here yesterday and what could I say?'

'She's . . . upset with me?'

'Really, Kenny! What can you expect her to think? One moment it's all on with you and the next you clear off without a word. Well, it just won't do. She's only human. And this time I'm afraid it was once too many.'

'Mum, I didn't mean to hurt her . . .'

'What's the use of saying that? It's the way you treat the poor girl that counts. And Joycey isn't a fool either, any more than your old mum.'

'Perhaps . . . she'll understand.'

'Don't count on that. She isn't wearing her ring any longer.'

'I'll talk to her. You'll see. But there's been . . . so much going on, lately.'

'Too much, my son.'

'Oh, mum! But there has, with one thing and another. There's all I'm going to do with the house, and then . . . well, that business in the forest.'

'Oh, that.'

Could he keep his voice steady? 'Have they . . . got any further with it yet?'

'Oh yes. They've got the bloke.'

'What!'

'It was in the paper this morning, the local press.'

He could feel the phone box in a whirl around him. 'But . . . who? Is it someone we know?'

'Nobody I know, but you might. It's someone who lives in your village.'

'Someone . . . !'

'Wait – I've got the paper here. It says his name is Jack Stringer, fifty-two, of Barn Cottage. Would you know him?'

'Bloody Biker!'

133

'Please, Kenny. Don't swear. Then you've met him?'

'But it frigging can't be!'

'Kenny, unless you stop swearing I shall hang up.'

'No mum – hang on!'

His legs were beginning to tremble. He shored himself up in the box, jammed the receiver to his ear with a shaking hand. 'You're sure – you're quite sure?'

'Yes. It's down here in black and white. Charged with the murder of a person unknown in Grimchurch Forest on 15 August. It's only a little bit in the stop-press, but it happened to catch my eye.'

'Jack Stringer!'

'That's the name.'

He held on tight. 'I know him, mum!'

'So I gather.'

'And I can't believe it . . . doesn't it say anything else at all?'

'Just what I told you.'

'But . . . how? I know he was around there at that time . . .'

'Well, that's it, then. You saw him there, did you?'

'Yes . . . I said in my statement . . . but I still can't see how!'

'Well, it's a bad business, son, and I can understand how you must feel. Especially if it's someone you know, someone you'd never guess would do such a thing. But that's how it is. These things do happen.'

'I know . . . but not him!'

'You'll just have to try and forget it, Kenny. Brooding over it isn't going to do you any good.'

'It must be a mistake!'

'Forget it, son. You know, I think it's time you came home.'

He sagged against the wall of the box. It couldn't be . . . it was impossible! A trick – a trap – they'd done it on purpose: a lousy trick to fetch him in! Biker . . . he was the last sodding person – how could they expect anyone to believe it? No, it was a feint. They'd arranged it with him . . . and he was stupid enough to let them do that!

'Are you still there?'

'Yes – yes, I'm here!'

'I'm afraid this has been a shock to you, son. And I don't like to think of you stuck away there with all this on your mind, it isn't right. Why don't you come home?'

'I can't – I can't, mum.'

'Why not. What's keeping you there?'

'Please, mum!'

'There's . . . nothing else, is there?'

'No! But things . . . I've got to think . . .' With an effort he hauled himself straighter. 'Look, mum, the money is running out! I'll be home soon, I really will, I won't stay here a minute longer than I have to. Only . . . not quite yet. I just need to be alone. And mum . . .'

'Son?'

'Mum, I love you!'

And the bloody pips went just then. Just as she was telling him she loved him too.

When he came out of the box he had to stand still for a minute to let the shakes drain from his body. He was near the camp-site and, when his legs felt steadier, he headed in that direction. Campers stared at him, kids broke off their game, a woman carrying a pail seemed about to speak to him. He went on through. Down to the lake shore. Slumped on the sward at the same spot as yesterday.

As yet he couldn't begin to think, could only sit there gazing at the lake. Birds flew by. A canoe passed. A dinghy was sailing towards picnic-island. Cloud bannered from the high tops and up there a bird like an eagle was soaring. It had to be real, yet, somehow, it wasn't, seemed just a dream going on about him. Was anything real? He let his eyes dazzle in the sunlight flashing from the wavelets . . .

Suppose – just suppose – it wasn't a trick!

It wouldn't be the first time such a thing had happened. Innocent men had been done up before and, in the old days, even hung . . .

And Biker, wasn't he just the sodding type, the sort of

135

weirdo they'd go after, a bloke who had never grown up but still acted like he was living in the Sixties? Yes, bloody yes – he might have been made for it! And the soft sod had admitted being around there. It could have happened. He could have seen that fellow and got an urge to prove bloody something . . .

Only that wasn't enough, they would need more than that to go on, a bit of evidence, a witness. Well then – the sodding traveller! Couldn't he have seen something that gave them a lead? Suppose Biker hadn't gone sailing past, had stopped for a word with the old bloke – and suppose the traveller had seen Biker with him. Wouldn't that be enough to do for the sod?

He picked up a pebble and slung it. And then – then – ?

But dare he think it?

Wasn't that just what they'd want him to be thinking, while all the bloody while . . .?

Lord Muck for one! He slung another pebble. Lord Muck wasn't one to be taken in. His eye was on Wicko, it would need more than the traveller to kid him that Biker was their man. He'd go along with it, oh yes, but only as a trap to catch a rabbit. A bit of bait for sodding Wicko, that's the way Lord Muck would play it.

And yet . . .

He slung several pebbles.

Would they, could they do that? Charge a man who they frigging knew . . . and put it in the papers, too?

If only he knew, if there was some bugger . . .

He held on to a pebble. Yes, there was one! Sid. Sid of the rotten Bell. Sid, who had all the gossip of the day . . .

Dare he risk it?

He hurled the pebble. Telephone enquiries would get him Sid's number. He was out of change, but that could be remedied, and now, before the bar opened . . .

He closed his eyes, sat a little longer, listened to the wavelets, the cries of children. It was no use – he would have to know! Finally, he dragged himself to his feet.

*

'Sid? It's Wicko.'

'Well, stone me! And where have you been hiding, mate?'

The nearest shop had been a tobacconist's, and though he didn't smoke he had bought some whiffs and a book of matches. He had paid with a note and, a little reluctantly, the tobacconist had made him change in coins. Now he was back again in the phone box, where enquiries had quickly put him through.

'I'm in . . . Torquay.'

'Torquay, is it? I wish I could sod off like you, mate! What sort of weather have you got down there? We've been having a damp spell here.'

'Here . . . it's fine.'

'Aren't you the lucky one! Found any decent skirt yet, Wicko?'

'Look, Sid – I'm in a box – and mum has just told me the news about Biker.'

'Oh . . . I see.' Sid paused: at once his tone had changed. 'Well there you are, what more can I tell you. It's been a shock to all of us round here.'

'But . . . when did it happen?'

'Yesterday, mate. They only pulled him in to check over his statement. And then it seemed the silly bugger confessed, or that's what a copper in here was telling us.'

'He confessed!'

'Would you credit it? And they hadn't got a thing on him. But that's how it was. He coughed his guts up. And this morning they had him in before the magistrates.'

'But . . . why did he confess?'

'Ask me another! He always was a soft sod.'

'And they believed him?'

'Must have done. He's sitting in a cell in Wolmering nick. You saw him around there that day, didn't you?'

'Yes – but!'

'That's all it needs, mate. They'll want you at the trial.'

'But – the gypo! Didn't he see him too?'

'Naow! He was down in the village, doing someone's garden. They've got another witness who saw Biker near the

137

forest, so you won't be alone up there in court.'

'And Lord – I mean the Chief Superintendent! He's quite happy about this?'

'Couldn't tell you, mate. He hasn't been down here. He was only giving our blokes a helping hand.'

'But wasn't he in charge?'

'No, not him. He'd have bigger fish to fry. But I dare say he'll have an opinion, if he's here at the weekend.'

The dial was near zero: Wicks jerked in a fresh coin.

'So it was . . . just our blokes on the job?'

'Why yes. And it was them he coughed to. I'll bet that's a feather in their caps.'

'The . . . soft sod.'

'You can say that again. Till yesterday, they didn't have a thing on him.'

'While now . . .'

'It's been a shock to everyone. But there you are, mate. Some bugger did it.'

'Yes. Some bugger . . .'

He leaned against the box. Still he couldn't quite take in the message, believe that all the torment he'd been going through was vain, his fears, his imaginings without foundation. Just two phone calls . . . and now! From a distance, he heard Sid's voice again.

'I don't want to rush you . . .'

'Sorry, Sid!'

'I'll be opening the bar in ten minutes. Was there anything else?'

'No Sid, that's all. What mum told me shook me and I thought I could get the low-down from you.'

'Well, that's the size of it, Wicko mate. So now you can get back to chasing the girls. When shall we see you again.'

'I . . . probably tomorrow!'

'I'll have a pint waiting. Watch your step!'

The phone went dead. It was some moments before he could bring himself to hang up. He was free . . . he was bloody free! Not even Lord Muck could drag him back to all that! His

138

head felt dizzy. He was himself again – Wicko, with his bloody millions behind him . . . Wicko, Wicko! Bloody shout it to the hills! Wicko, with the sodding world before him . . .

'Will fifties be all right, sir?'

The bank was the first place had gone to, the big one, in the high street, the one with the gilt-framed double doors. Too long he'd been conscious of that limp wallet and its lean wafer of tens – it wasn't Wicko! And he ignored the bloody cash-points. He wanted some real money, him. So he'd scribbled a cheque at one of the tables and presented it at the counter with his card . . . and even then the frigging clerk had made him wait while he rang for authorization!

'No. Give me tens.'

'It's rather a large sum, sir . . .'

'Tens, I said!'

'Well, I'll just see . . .'

He had to borrow from the next till, but finally the sum was counted out – a fat, fat bunch of notes that almost over-whelmed Wicks's wallet. So who cared? Some he stuffed in his pocket! And he could feel the weight of that wallet again. It was Wicko, the real Wicko, who was pushing out through those swing doors . . .

His next move was predictable: also occupying the lake shore was a hotel, the John Peel Arms, a large, old-fashioned-looking place with a sprinkling of up-market cars on its gravel. The best place in town? It bloody looked like it! He crunched past the cars and went in. A smart little blonde doll in reception looked up to greet him with a cautious smile.

'Is lunch on, miss?'

'In half an hour, sir. But you'll find the bar open.'

'Would you by any chance have a room?'

'I'll just look . . . we get rather full at this time of year, sir!'

But of course there was one, and a bloody good one – it had a view down the lake, a poncey *en suite*, telly, drinks cabinet, phone.

'I'll take it.'

'We charge seventy-five, sir. But lunch and the evening-meal are extra.'

'For one night.'

'Very good, sir. Now, if you will just sign the book . . .'

Not only did he sign it, but made a point of writing his address in full, post-code and all – what did he have to fear now? Then he sauntered into the bar and drank a scotch along with the tweedies, gave an eye to the comely barmaid, even ventured on a whiff. He was back. He was back! He was out from bloody under. Life was on again. The sun was shining. He had as much right there as the best of them . . .

Salmon, grouse, Black Forest and a bottle of the best they had. After lunch he strolled back to the pub to collect his gear and the Jag. That lousy room! How had he stood it? Not so much a room as a prison cell. It needed only bars across the little window, a sodding peep-hole in the door. He grabbed his gear together quickly and went down to the bar to pay.

'Changed your mind then, have you?'

'Looks like it.'

'Nothing to do with last night, is it?'

'Sod last night!'

'Well, you know best, mate! But that'll be another twenty quid . . .'

He slung his bag in the Jag and set it drifting. Now, now he was clear of the last of it. The loneliness. The fear. The shrinking notes in his wallet. And none of it had mattered, it had been an illusion, a nightmare he had dreamed up for himself! A couple of phone calls had been all it needed to drag him back out of the pit . . . He could talk to mum again. Gweny. Joycey. The road back home lay open before him . . .

His mind was still in a daze when he parked the Jag on the John Peel gravel, and after taking his bag to his room he strolled down the hotel's lawn to the edge of the lake. He found a garden-bench and sat. The lake lay placid in a flat calm. Afternoon sun was shadowing the peaks and casting shade from the shrubs beside it. He lit another whiff, watched the smoke rise from it. Behind him, some of the guests were playing tennis. Frigging peace ... frigging normality! But could he really, really believe ...? It had been too sudden. One moment despair, the next an answer to every question ... couldn't it still be a trap, a web of deceit they were closing round him? Biker's confession – dare he credit it? Well, he was the sort of drip who might make one, a loner, an eccentric, a bloke who might think the notoriety worth it. And they had charged him, had him up before the beaks ... he must have made that confession stick. Would they dare do that, unless ...? Wicks found himself shaking his head. It was bloody geniune. Had to be. And with Lord Muck apparently out of the picture ...

'Seen a ball come this way, old fruit?'

No – he hadn't!

'No need to get shirty ...'

A young fool in flannel shorts: he was poking around the shrubs with his racket. Then he found his sodding ball, took himself off back to the tennis-court ...

Genuine: it had to be genuine! All they wanted him for was to be a witness. He had seen Biker, that's all he had to say, and it was up to the jury what they made of that ... Even, it might be, that Biker would get off – stranger things than that had happened. And ... if he didn't? Well, the soft sod had asked for it and he couldn't hang that round Wicko's neck!

He stared at the lake. At the hills.

Yes ... yes! He could safely accept it.

He could go back. He could ring mum, tell her that tomorrow he would be on his way ...

He went up over the lawn again, past the tennis-players, into the hotel.

'Mum?'

'Oh, it's you again, Kenny.'

'Mum, I'll be home again tomorrow. You can expect me about tea-time. I may be there a little sooner.'

'This is very sudden, son.'

'I've been thinking about what you said to me, mum. And

141

you're right. I need to be at home. To have you and everyone round me.'

'Well, I can't say I'm not glad. But are you sure you mean it, son?'

'Yes, mum. I've been behaving like a fool. But everything is going to be all right now.'

'Don't forget, then. And as soon as you're back here – '

'I know, mum! I'll call on you first thing.'

'Well, as long as you remember.'

'It's a promise. And mum?'

'Yes?'

'I do still love you!'

He hung up. Now the die was cast . . . He stared down at the tennis-players. Tomorrow, it was this that would be the dream, a dream left somewhere across England. He had wanted to tell mum where he was, to stir those memories of far-off times. Perhaps later he would . . . But, just now, what he wanted most was a tot from the drinks cabinet.

What a bloody day!

Later he tried to ring Gweny, but the phone rang in an empty house.

10

'Keep the change.'

'Are you sure, sir . . .?'

That morning there had been a heavy mist on the lake.
From the window of his room he could barely make out the
silhouettes of the trees on picnic-island. Nor had it lifted, two
hours later, when he went out to the dewy Jag. Alone, the
peak of the great mountain behind the town appeared spectre-
like through the haze.

'A bit of a thick one, sir! Have you far to go?'

The previous evening, before dinner, he had taken a stroll
in the town, and there, at a souvenir shop that was still open,
had bought trinkets to take back for mum and Gweny. Then,
after dinner and a couple of pints, he had retired to his room
and the TV. Suddenly he was feeling weary, a tiredness that
invaded his every limb: he fell asleep in the middle of the
news . . . but what would there have been in that for him?
And so to bed, and dreamless sleep till the phone rang with
his early call. Was he fully awake yet? His mind felt empty,
his responses mechanical.

'Shouldn't be too much traffic mid-week, sir.'

With an effort, he set the Jag rolling over the gravel. The
John Peel, the town, vanished from his mirror, road stretched
before him, the road pointing towards the east. Was he doing
the right thing? It was too late now! His course was set and he
knew it. Road was going to lead to road until . . .

He switched on the radio, but didn't take it in: background
voices that said nothing. He was driving with lights through

the mist that still persisted, his speed no more than fifty. This time the Dales could go stuff themselves, he was sticking to main roads all the way ... across the Pennines to Scotch Corner, down the gruesome A1, Newark, the Fens ... In conditions like this, would he make it? The rotten mist showed no sign of lifting. Over the Pennines it would probably get worse, and things never improved on the A1 ... In addition he was short of flaming juice, would have to waste time at some service station. He glanced at the gauge – yes! He should have filled the tank up before he left ...

Frustratedly, he stabbed at the radio till voices gave way to a blare of pop. Was he – was he really doing the right thing? Shouldn't he have stayed clear till the fuss had dried up? They had got Biker in a cell, true, but the sod might have a change of heart – he had had his moment of glory! Any time at all he could withdraw that confession. They might not accept it, but it would set them thinking, and with Lord Muck holding their hands ... And it wasn't too late. They could place him where he'd been, but the rest of the country was wide open to him ...

Only ... now he had promised mum.

He stabbed the radio again, got an American voice talking politics.

Mum. She was expecting him, waiting for him, probably had a meal planned for that evening.

No, he couldn't chicken out now.

He had made his sodding bed and he would have to lie on it ...

He hooted a car that had overtaken him – a lousy ten-year-old Fiesta! His foot itched, but he managed to control it. Some stupid young fool out to prove something ...

Meanwhile the American had got on to baseball: another stab brought him classical music.

He set his teeth tight and drove on. Perhaps, after all, he was doing the best thing he could. To show up there as though he didn't give a damn, had nothing to fear, couldn't bloody care less. If Biker recanted, so what? All they had on Wicko

144

was that he was a witness. If they had accepted Biker's tale – and they had – then they could have nothing that implicated himself. Suspect they might – rotten Lord Muck would! But proof they didn't have a smell of . . .

No. No. Keep driving, Wicko. Keep right on down that road. Lord Muck you may have to outstare, but that's the long and the bloody short . . .

He picked up petrol at the next row of pumps and settled down to the long haul. By mid-morning he had seen off the Pennines and was belting down the A1. The jam was still there – what else? – but today it held him up a bare half-hour, and by lunch-time he was able to check in at a Little Chef at the right end of the A1(M). Bloody progress! He lingered over lunch, had a second go at the maple-syrup pancakes.

'Keep the change.'

Now it looked like rain: the mist he had left behind at Wetherby. But at Newark he was quitting the A1, was beginning to head straight and true for home. Not so much further . . . The Sleaford bypass hastened him into sight of the Fens, the great levels, dark now under cloud, and the final stride between him and his goal. So different from the country he had left behind! But beginning to be the country where he belonged . . . East country, where roads were flat and houses no longer built of stone. The rain began at Sutton Bridge and never left him after that. The sodden Fens led to sodden Norfolk and then to his own rainswept county. What did it matter? He was nearly back! Now the rain was his own rain . . .

By six he had made it, was turning into Pier Avenue, with familiar houses all around him. And there was a light showing in the hall of the bungalow when he parked the Jaguar at the gate. How many miles? He couldn't bother to check. He switched off engine, radio, lights. The rain pelted on him when he got out and he ran the last few yards to the door of the bungalow.

*

145

'Do wipe your feet, Kenny, please! I only hoovered the hall this morning.'

Would he have wanted any other greeting at the end of his savage journey? The place was right, the smell was right and he could see the table already laid. Home ... home ... he was bloody home! And he wiped his feet with officious care.

'There ... that's better! Did you have rain all the way up here? When I saw it I thought you might be late, so I cooked a hot-pot just in case.'

'Yes ... it's been raining.'

'Let me see you, son. You don't look well. Is there anything wrong?'

'No, nothing, mum! I'm just tired.'

'Well, you're not much of an advert for Torquay! You had better come in and sit down.'

'Yes ... thanks.'

'I suppose it's that business in the forest that's been getting to you.'

He followed her into the parlour and sat. Oh hell, if he could only have told her! It was poised on the tip of his tongue, urging him to blurt it out. Would she have stood by him? He knew she would, but only if he faced up and went straight to the police ... to cover for him wasn't in her nature. Tell mum and tell the world ...

'Kenny, just look at it like this. What's done is done and can never be undone. It was a terrible thing, I know, and the worse for you knowing the man who did it. But it wasn't your fault. You couldn't have stopped him. You simply mustn't go blaming yourself. You assisted the police when they asked you and now you've just got to try to put it behind you. Isn't that common sense?'

'Yes, mum!'

'Then face up to it, son. Stop looking so hang-dog.'

'I'm ... trying.'

'I don't know, really! Sometimes I wouldn't know you for a

146

son of mine. You've been having proper meals have you, down there?'

'Yes.'

'Then try to look more cheerful, while I go to serve up.'

He glared at the table. Why go on trying? Were things ever going to be the same again? Even if they did Biker he would have to go on living with it, and on top of it the knowledge that the bugger was inside ... Things might go on, but they couldn't be the same. Not with Gweny. With Joycey. Mum. He would be acting the same part as he was now, today, tomorrow ... for frigging ever! Clear out? Get away? But he felt himself shrink from it. Somehow ... some bloody how ...

'Joyce was here, Kenny.'

He didn't respond.

'I told her you might be back today. I would have had her come in and join us, but of course this is Wednesday and she's on late. But she does want to see you, son, and if you take my advice you won't hang about.'

'Perhaps ... tomorrow.'

'Yes, that's her half-day. Take her somewhere quiet in the country, Kenny. Then you could bring her back here and we could talk things over.'

'Well ... if she wants to.'

'I'm sure she does. I was having a word with her mother about it.'

He stirred in the chair – dad's chair! Was anything like it still possible? For an instant he conjured up a vision of that face, the eyes softening, felt the warmth of her body pressing to his. Yes ... it might be! It could yet be the way. The despair that now froze him didn't have to be for ever. If he just kept the ball rolling, playing it her way, mum's way, then life, the moment, might return to him again ...

'Give her a ring when she gets in, son.'

'Yes ... I'll do that, mum.'

'Of course, she won't want to see you tonight, but you can

147

fix something up. I'm sure she'll like that. And son, give Gweny a ring. She's full of ideas about the house.'

'I will, mum.'

'Then we can talk it over. Perhaps Joyce will have ideas about it too.'

The hot-pot arrived, the veg, the pudding. He did his best to eat up as she expected. For a spell there was silence while they dealt with the food, but he could feel her eyes watching him, solemn, concerned. Bloody hell ... it couldn't have altered him so much! The face he'd seen when he shaved that morning had still been Wicko's. Over the pudding, with an effort, he caught her eye, forcing himself to make a smile.

'That's better! You like your ginger pud?'

'No one makes them like you do, mum.'

'I know, that's what your father used to say. You must remind me to give Joyce the recipe.'

'Perhaps you'll come and make us one at the house.'

She shook her head gaily. 'Oh no, my son! Your Joyce won't want me interfering there. That's a sure way for a mother-in-law to make herself unwanted. Besides, I don't know your kitchen.'

'You could get to know it, mum.'

'Oh no. I'll come only as a guest, and when you ask me.'

'But ... later on?'

Now her headshake was firm. 'You can put those ideas away, my man. This is my home and it's going to stay so. I'm never going to be a nuisance to my children.'

'But you wouldn't be a nuisance!'

'Oh yes I would. When I do things, I do them my way. And why would you want me to leave this place, where you all grew up, and which is your home too?'

'We could keep it on ...'

'Forget it, Kenny. When I leave this place it will be in a box. This is the house your dad bought for us and you'll never persuade me to go anywhere else.'

'But I may never marry bloody Joyce!'

'Don't swear, Kenny. And it makes no difference. If you

want to, you can come back here, but don't ask me to move to that house of yours.'

And she began gathering the dishes together, her face set, her mouth a thin line. Mum . . . He jammed his plates together, reached for hers, followed her into the kitchen.

'Mum . . . I'm sorry!'

'It's all right, Kenny.'

'I don't want us to quarrel, mum. But sometimes . . . I mean, there's all this money. And you won't let me do anything for you.'

'You've given the girls some.'

'But not you!'

'Son, I've got everything I need.'

'It couldn't hurt you – a bit in your account.'

She rested the dishes, sighed, looked up at him. Then shook her head sadly. 'Son, when I see what it's done to you! Often, I wish you had never won that money. Sometimes I wonder if it's still my boy when I look at you and hear you talk. Will you ever be my Kenny again, the young man I was once so proud of?'

'Mum – oh, mum!'

She stared very intently. 'There's something wrong, isn't there, Kenny? It isn't just what that man did in the forest. It's something that goes much deeper than that.'

'Mum, you're imagining things!'

'Am I? Look me straight in the eye and tell me again.'

'Mum . . . you're imagining it!'

She stared long, then sighed again. 'Well. Perhaps I am.'

The plates were trembling. He put them down. 'Mum, it's going to be all right. Nothing has happened, I'm still your son, and Joycey . . . everything. It's going to work.'

'And . . . you've nothing to tell me?'

'No! I may have been a bit wild, but nothing else. And that's all over, I'm putting it behind me. From now on things are really going to change.'

'I've heard you say that before, son.'

'This time I mean it, believe me. You're going to be proud

149

of me again, mum. All the things you want for me are going to come true.'

Did he mean that? Yes – yes, he did! It was the way, the only way. Forget the rest, bloody forget it: just go on seeing things through mum's eyes . . .

'I want to be proud of you, son.'

'You will be!'

'I'm just afraid . . .'

'Mum, there's no need. That trip I made was the last kick. Now I've come to my senses.'

She gazed up at him. Her eyes were wet. She held out her arms. 'Oh, Kenny!'

'Oh, mum!'

He hugged her to him and kissed her. As she'd always done, since he was a kid, she ran her hand over his hair.

'And you'll be ringing Joycey?'

'Yes. I promise.'

'She won't be home till after ten.'

'After ten, then.'

Slowly, she released herself. 'Coffee?'

'I think I'd sooner have tea.'

After the washing-up, she let him go, coming to the door to watch him leave. The rain had stopped, but cloud was still heavy with the promise of more to come. He belted himself in, started the engine, looked back at mum silhouetted in the doorway. She raised her hand, he raised his too. She was still waving hers as he drove away.

Was it really going to work . . .?

He drove slowly along the wet Front, paused by the lighthouse, whose measured flashes were blazing against the stormy sky. There would be pitfalls in plenty. He would need to watch his every step. Mum was sharp, and so was Joycey, they could spot a lie before he spoke it. But . . . if he could get this other business behind him . . . or at least, not let it show . . .? Then, then there was hope, a glimpse of a future beyond all this . . .

He drove back through the town, past the supermarket

where Joycey worked. He glanced across at the lit windows, but all he saw there were the shoppers with their trolleys.

His wipers were going by the time he reached the village, and the green stretched deserted down to the pond and its line of trees. He parked in the road, not in the drive, and hesitated before switching off his lights – let the sods see that Wicko was back! He hung on for a minute before going in. As at mum's, the door opened on a smell, but here it was an odour that offered no welcome. Not all of Vera's ministrations could get rid of that breath of age and dissolution. He found some mail she had picked up on the hall cabinet and took it through with him to the lounge. There he switched on the TV before sprawling on the comfortless settee.

His house!

He gazed around him. What the bloody hell was he doing here?

If he spent every last sodding penny he'd got he could never bring life back to this place.

It belonged to the past, old people, old times, and even then it must have been a penance to live there. It would have needed servants, gardeners, a whole frigging staff . . . it would have been like living in an institution. And mum knew it. One glance had told her. It was a sodding house, but it could never be a home. Dazzled by his money, her stupid son had bought it, but no way was he ever going to make it his own. Why couldn't he have seen that?

The television was crap. He looked at the letters he still held in his hand. One was from an interior designer, the other from a garden centre. He threw them aside. No . . . that was all over! Tomorrow he'd put the rotten place on the market. Joycey would understand. She'd even be relieved . . . What they needed was something modern, say a super-super-exec, more like one of those across the green . . .

He squashed the TV, went back to the hall, picked up the telephone and dialled.

151

'Gweny . . .?'

'Well, well! Is that my long-lost brother I can hear?'

'Gweny, listen – '

'Are you home by any chance – or are you still dazzling them down in Torquay?'

'I'm home, but – '

'What went wrong? Did they toss you out of your hotel again?'

'Gweny, please listen!'

'I can't think why I should bother, when you've got so very little time for yours truly. You want something, do you?'

'Gweny, I'm sorry!'

He heard her grunt. 'And so you should be, Kenneth Wicks! When I've been wasting so much time on your behalf and you can't even bring yourself to keep in touch. So what is it now?'

'I just thought I should tell you – '

'Yes?'

'Well . . . I've changed my mind about this place. I'm going to sell it. I think it's better if I have somewhere more like yours.'

At the other end, a pause. 'Have you gone bonkers?'

'Gweny, listen – '

'No, you listen to me! If ever you dream of selling that place, Kenny, I'll never speak to you again.'

'But it's in such a mess, Gweny . . .'

'I don't care. It isn't as though you didn't have the means. And with Dick and me to help you, you can turn that house into a show-place. Don't you realize what you've got there?'

'Yes . . . but!'

'It's a lovely period piece, Kenny. You've got a responsibility to it. You took it on and now you've got to go through with it. So no more talk about selling. Are you with me?'

'It's just too much, Gweny!'

'Utter rot, my little brother. And before you hang up on me, I'm coming over tomorrow to see what really needs doing. Are you hearing me?'

'Yes . . . yes.'

'I'll be over there at ten. And I'll expect you to be there, so don't try to oil out.'

'I'll . . . be there.'

'Just see you are. Really, Kenny, you should be in a home.'

He slammed the phone down. Why? Why? Perhaps he should make her a present of the place! She wasn't living in it, didn't know, was still seeing it as some sort of dream palace. And she bloody meant it. She wouldn't let him back out; tomorrow she'd have him signing something . . . might even bring people along with her, make sodding certain he was in the trap! Well, he had had his warning, hadn't he? And the Jag was still parked outside . . .

He returned to the lounge and switched on the news, but all they could talk about was rotten Ireland. Did someone care? He changed channels, got a sodding police-drama, and quickly switched off.

They would want to see him, he knew that, he was a bloody star witness.

Tomorrow some time, there'd be a knock on the door, and there the lousy fellow would stand.

Could he go through with it? He would have to! Biker was inside and there he must stay. He didn't have to accuse the bloke, just give his testimony, let them make what they wanted of that . . .

Too bloody bad! But he had brought it on himself. And Wicko would be a fool to feel guilt about that. A soft sod who'd jumped at his moment of glory, the local headlines, perhaps a mention on TV. No, he had chosen the part and didn't give a crap that someone outside . . .

Wicks glared at the blank screen. Dare he, dare he be so certain? Certain that . . . But bloody yes! It was too late now to start having doubts. He was clear. There was nothing on him. He had only got to go on playing his part. In a few minutes he'd be ringing Joycey, making arrangements, ringing mum . . .

153

Then he heard a knock at the door. And he was on his feet like a jack-rabbit.

'Oh . . . it's you, Vera.'

'I saw your car, Mr Kenny. I thought I would just run across and see how you were getting on. Did you have a good time in Torquay?'

'I . . . yes.'

'I thought about you, down there. I was there myself once, on a coach-tour. All those palm trees and that. May I come in?'

He stood back for her to enter.

'There's something else I had to tell you, but that will keep. Would you like me to make you a nice pot of tea?'

He didn't, really. He could have done without Vera. But he let her go through and plug in the kettle. In short order she had a tea-tray laid and was rummaging in a cupboard for biscuits.

'Your mother rang me – did you know? It was rather naughty of you, Mr Kenny! You forgot to tell her where you were off to and she was a little put out by that. Have you seen her?'

'Yes . . . I called in. Everything is all right now, Vera.'

'That's good, Mr Kenny. Your sister came looking for you, too.'

'I've just rung her.'

'She's a nice girl. She said she was going to help you with the house.'

Almost, he was grinding his teeth!

'Shall I pour here, or bring it through?'

'This will do.'

'I saw your car earlier, but Mrs Tungate was with me, watching TV.'

He took his tea. Couldn't she understand that he was in no mood for bloody housekeepers? Apparently not. She sat down with her cup and seemed prepared to chatter on . . .

154

'Now – what I had to tell you, Mr Kenny!'

'Vera, it's been a long day . . .'

'Oh dear, I'm sorry – and me rabbiting on! So I'll just tell you this and then I'll go.' She gave him an arch little look. '*He* was here, Mr Kenny. You know. The one who lives at Heatherings. He called here after lunch, hoping to have a word with you.'

Tea slopped in his cup. 'He . . . what?'

'I know! I was just as surprised as you are. I was only across here to pick up your mail and see that everything was in order. And then he knocked on the door.'

'And . . . you let him in?'

'Well, I had to, Mr Kenny. We couldn't stand talking on the doorstep. And I'd just got the kettle on.'

He managed to ground the trembling cup. 'And . . .?'

'Seems they need you as a witness – you know! So I had to tell him that you were in Torquay and showed him that note. He asked if he could keep it.'

'He – kept the note?'

'Yes. He was awfully nice, Mr Kenny! He asked all about you, whether you often went off on trips like this. Of course, I told him you didn't, there'd only been that weekend in London, and you hadn't thought much of that – you came back in quite a way, if you remember.'

'You . . . told him . . . that?'

'Well, where was the harm? He was so understanding, it was a pleasure to talk to him. And he may be able to do you a bit of good, Mr Kenny. Didn't you burn some old papers before you left?'

His hands were crushing the chair. 'Papers . . .?'

'Yes, in the fireplace in the sitting-room. I knew they weren't there the day before, because that's when I did it out. Well, he saw them there, and poked them around, and do you know what? He found a bit of a banknote! It must have been among the papers you burned, and he asked me for a bag and took the ashes away. So you could get your money back, Mr Kenny. It seems the banknote was a big one.'

155

He could feel the scream exploding inside him, but some-how, somehow he was keeping it down. The chair was creaking under his hands, he had to jam his teeth to prevent them chattering. And the bitch was giggling!

'Do you know what, Mr Kenny? He asked me if you ever paid me in fifty-pound notes! Well, I had to tell him, of course. You did offer me one once, but I had to turn it down. I mean, what would they have said at the shop if they'd had to give me change for a note that size? Mr Kenny? Are you all right?'

He didn't scream then, either! 'Vera . . .'

'Yes?'

'Just . . . leave me, Vera.'

'But Mr Kenny . . .'

'Just bloody leave me!'

She started up, alarmed. 'Well . . . if that's what you want.'

She stared at him a moment with fearful eyes. Then grabbed her headscarf. And hurriedly left.

He smashed something, he didn't remember what, and then he was back in the sodding car. Moments after that he was in the Bell, where Sid was tidying up the glasses before closing.

'What sort of time . . .'

'Was he in here – was the bastard asking about me?'

'Hold hard now!'

'About the bloody notes!'

'Look – '

'Was he?'

'So what if he was?'

'And you frigging told him?'

'See here, old partner! I'm not sure I like your attitude. But if I did tell him, so what? It can't matter now, when they've got Biker . . .'

His fingers itched. 'I should do you up!'

'Look, any more of that talk and I'm ringing the police!'

'So bloody ring them!'

'I just may do that . . .'

And then he was outside again, by the lousy pond, where a startled duck quacked at him and drips from the trees fell on his head. How long was he standing there? Christ knew! Christ knew why he was there at all. Or any frigging where – what was the sense? What? What?

'Wicko . . . so you're back with us!'

The sodding tart must have crept up on him.

'Get in the car, you!'

'You sure you're in the mood, lover-boy?'

'Get in!'

'How can a girl refuse?'

He didn't quite shove her into the Jag, but he slammed the door after her. The next moment he was beside her, had her body leaning against his. He could see the glimmer of her face by the light that still shone above the door of the Bell.

'I've been wanting a word with you, lover. That bloke from the Yard has been around. Oh, don't worry! I told him nothing. But I got this bloody impression.'

Was it ice in his veins or blood? 'What did the bugger want to know?'

'I'll let you guess. Whether I knew you and, you know, whether I'd heard any wild talk.'

'But . . .?'

'What do you think, lover-boy? I know when to keep my mouth shut. But I tell you, I got this impression. I don't think he's happy with Biker.'

'Not . . .?'

She shook her head. 'So, a word to the wise, lover. Watch your tongue. If you don't you could make it awkward for yourself.'

He sat rigid. She wriggled against him. His fingers were wrenching at the wheel. Then he heard the sound of the car engine, saw the lights pulling in behind him.

'Who – ?'

But he bloody knew, had the engine rolling in a moment. He was in gear, brakes off, when the frigger came running, waving him to stop. Squealing tyres, a yelp from the tart and

157

the bugger standing helpless, watching them go. Standing helpless – bloody Lord Muck! But then he was belting towards the pub, the phone . . .

'Did you have to . . .!'

Yes, he had to!

'That was him, wasn't it?'

He drove, he drove. The village vanished, the roads untangled, he was back on the sodding A road. The bitch beside him was moaning, squawking when he slid on a bend.

'Wicko, you're drunk!'

Oh no he wasn't!

'Wicko, it's you he's after, isn't it?'

If he could catch him, bloody catch him . . . and there was a chance, still one more chance!

'I'm frightened, Wicko!'

'This'll do . . .'

An empty lay-by yawned on the left. He braked, tyres screeching, jammed the Jag in under the trees. He snapped the seat-belt the bitch had plugged in.

'No Wicko, no – not here . . .!'

His hands were on her, tight, tight, her eyes staring out of her head. Now, now! He thrust her out, saw the limp body roll in the mud. Then the slamming door, the roar of the engine, the road leaping to meet him again. No tales to tell there! And for the rest . . . still in the back his frigging bag! Drive, Wicko, drive. Keep the bloody road coming . . .

He heard the siren. He didn't care! Under his bonnet he had the answer. Drive, drive, and the sodding siren fading away, fading behind him. No contest! The flickering needle leant away across the dial. Lights were shooting by him like comets, stragglers he picked off as though shelling nuts.

Wicko, Wicko!

Wicko in the stars . . .

Lights in groups, single lights.

Lights. Lights. Lights.

And then the biggest lights of all . . .

The note of the siren grew stronger again, grew to a

crescendo, died away to a wail. Doors slammed, feet came running, voices shouted. But Wicko didn't hear.

Meanwhile, in the lay-by a few miles back, the prostitute Sandra stirred, and groaned.

Brundall, 1994–95